LASSIE
The Wild
Mountain Trail

LASSIE

THE WILD MOUNTAIN TRAIL

AUTHORIZED EDITION

by I. G. EDMONDS

Illustrated by
LARRY HARRIS

WHITMAN PUBLISHING COMPANY • Racine, Wisconsin

Contents

1 Mystery at Black Rock

PAUL CARTER put his suitcase down and looked about with dismay. Behind him the train started to pull away from the Black Rock station on the edge of Blue River National Forest.

"Isn't there *anybody* to meet me?" he said aloud, looking uneasily down the town's single street.

There was a ghost-town look about Black Rock. In the two years Paul had been away to school, many of the stores had closed. Their broken windows and sagging doors added to the shadow of sadness that hung over the dying town. The only living thing Paul could see was a beautiful collie dog bounding up the central street toward the train station.

7

Paul only glanced at the dog and then looked across the tree-covered mountains in the direction of his mother's ranch, which bordered the national forest on the north. Dark clouds hugged the distant ridges. Haze softened them so he could not tell if they were storm clouds or the smoke of a forest fire.

"I hope it isn't a fire," Paul said to himself. As a person raised in the forest, Paul dreaded fire, but it did make him feel better to think there might be a reason no one from the ranch had come to meet him.

He picked up the suitcase and started to enter the station. The collie he had seen in the street came bounding across the platform. She skidded to a stop and raised a white paw for him to shake.

Paul grinned and stooped to shake the dog's paw. She was tawny with a snow-white ruff and a thin blaze down her graceful head.

"What is your name, girl?" he asked. "I'm Paul Carter. You must be new around here.

You weren't here when I went off to school."

The collie barked eagerly. Paul smiled and got up.

"You know," he said, looking down at the dog's eager face, "I think you really believe you can talk! Sorry I haven't the time to visit with you, girl, but I have to find a way home."

He started into the station and almost collided with an elderly man who was hurrying out.

The old man jumped back and blinked at Paul in surprise.

"Sam!" Paul cried. "Sam Gresham! Don't you remember me?"

"Paul! Paul Carter!" the old man cried. "I didn't see you get off the train."

"I broke the catch on my suitcase. By the time I got it fixed the train was pulling out. I got off just in time."

"I was loading the mail sacks," Sam Gresham said. "That's why I didn't see you."

"It's wonderful to be back in the forest,

Sam," Paul said happily, breathing deeply of the bracing mountain air. "Towns are for town people."

"Ain't it the truth!" the old man cried. "The only skyscraper I have any use for is a tall old sugar pine reaching right up to heaven."

"I feel the same way," Paul replied. "But tell me, Sam, is that a fire over toward the ranch?"

He pointed toward the cloud hugging the distant ridge.

Sam Gresham looked uneasy. It struck Paul that the old man did not want to talk about the fire. This puzzled Paul. Sam was one of the best-liked men in the mountains. It was not like him to be evasive.

Finally Sam said, "Well, I suppose it is a fire." Then he added quickly, "But it isn't much of one. Corey Stuart called a half-hour ago to say it was under control. Corey is the new ranger who came about six months after you left for school. He's a fine man. You'll like him,

Paul—no question about it."

"I guess the fire is the reason no one from the ranch came in to meet me," Paul said.

The smile that came to Sam's face when he spoke of Corey Stuart vanished when Paul mentioned the fire again. "I guess that is the reason," he said glumly. "The roads are closed up your way."

"I'm surprised Hardrock didn't come anyway," Paul said. "I could just see him saddling old Comstock and coming across the hills. He never had any use for roads anyway."

"Well—" Sam said uncertainly. "I—uh—suppose so. . . ."

"Sam!" Paul's explosive cry made the old man jump. "What's wrong?"

"Why—uh—why do you ask that?" Sam asked evasively.

"Has something happened to Hardrock?"

Sam looked as if it pained him to speak. "Well, I guess it has, Paul," he said sadly.

"Why didn't you say so?" Paul exclaimed in

sudden fear. "What is all the mystery about?"

"Well, for one thing," Sam said, "he had a bad fall up in the Wild Mountain area."

"Oh, no!" Paul cried. "Is he dying?"

"No! No! Nothing like that," Sam said hastily.

Paul let out a sigh of relief. Hardrock Hartley had pretty much taken the place of the boy's father, who had died when Paul was three. There was no man Paul admired more.

In the beginning it had been hero worship of a small boy for the man who taught him woodcraft. Then as Paul grew into his teens he began to realize the wonderful character of the old prospector.

Life had not treated Hardrock Hartley kindly. But years of reverses had not changed the old man's often-voiced belief that "a man's bound to win if he's right and keeps on fighting."

"Is Hardrock in the hospital?" Paul asked.

"No," Sam said, still seeming reluctant to

talk about their friend. "He was, but he—got out."

There was genuine suffering in the baggage-man's face. Paul knew what good friends Sam and Hardrock were. Suddenly he wondered if the fall had crippled the old prospector. To men who loved the outdoors as Sam and Hard-rock did, that would be worse than death. He decided not to pain Sam any more by pressing him with questions.

"I need a way to get home. Could you—"

The shrill ring of a phone inside the bag-gage room interrupted their conversation. Sam seemed relieved to go answer it.

Paul heard him say, "Oh! It's you, Corey. No, those two junior foresters you were ex-pecting weren't on the train. . . . That's too bad. . . . Sure, the railroad has some extra shovels. . . . You bet your life we'll loan them to you. . . . Wait a minute, will you, Corey?"

Sam turned to Paul. "Can you drive a pick-up?" he asked.

"Sure," Paul said.

"Fine," Sam replied and turned his head back to the phone. "You won't have to lose any time coming in for the shovels, Corey. Paul Carter is here. He can drive the pickup out."

Then Sam was silent, listening to the Forest Service man at the other end of the line.

"Oh," Sam said in reply to Corey Stuart. "That's right; you don't know him. His mother owns the ranch across the hogback from the government land. Paul's been away to school. He just came in on the train. He'll bring the pickup out with the shovels. Then you can drive him on home. Okay?"

He listened to Mr. Stuart's reply and then handed the phone to Paul. "Corey wants to talk to you," he said. "He took over as district forest ranger when Tom Cooley retired. Everybody likes him as much as they did Tom."

Paul took the telephone receiver. He heard a deep, friendly voice say, "Welcome home, Paul. Do you think you can drive out the pickup for me? I don't want to leave here until I'm sure the fire will not jump the breaks."

"Sure thing, Mr. Stuart," Paul said quickly. He had always admired the outdoorsmen of the Forest Service, and he was tickled at the opportunity to help them. "I know the roads."

"Well, that's one of the troubles," Corey Stuart said. "The roads are out. You'll have to drive up one of the firebreak lanes. It will be easy to get lost, but I think Lassie can keep you going straight."

"Lassie?" Paul asked.

"Yes, she came into Black Rock with me early this morning. I had an unexpected load of material that came in on the first train. I left her in town, intending to pick her up when I came in later."

"Okay," Paul said. "I'll bring her out."

"She'll set you right if you make a wrong turn."

"I'll make it," Paul said, somewhat resentful of Corey's thinking a girl knew more about these mountains than he did.

"Good," Corey said. "Just take things easy. You will be driving over some pretty rough trails. But unless the fire makes an unexpected break, there'll be no danger. If that happens, I'll send someone to head you off."

After admonishing Paul to turn back if he should encounter any fire danger, Corey Stuart hung up. Paul turned to Sam.

"He said Lassie would show me the way," Paul said. "Is Lassie Mr. Stuart's daughter?"

Sam chuckled. "I'll show you who Lassie is," he said. He raised his voice to a shout. "Lassie! Come here, girl!"

A few seconds later the collie Paul had left on the station platform bounded into the baggage room. She sat down and again raised a white paw for Paul to shake. Her plumed tail beat a friendly tattoo on the floor. Paul looked at her in astonishment.

"Shake hands with Lassie, Paul," Sam said with a grin.

"We've already shaken hands," Paul said, recovering from his surprise.

"Well, shake her hand again and you'll know her twice as well!" Sam said brightly.

Paul grinned and stooped to shake Lassie's paw. The collie barked happily.

"She's taken quite a shine to you, Paul," Sam said, fondly scratching Lassie's head.

"She's a pretty dog," Paul replied. "But surely Mr. Stuart was joking about her showing me the way to the fire camp."

"Nope. Lassie is your guide."

Paul looked at his old friend in dismay. He knew the firebreaks were just strips hewn out of the wild brush. He also knew how difficult it would be to follow these strips across the mountains.

"But Lassie is just a *dog!*" he protested. "How can she keep me from turning down the wrong lane?"

"Lassie has more sense than most people I've met," Sam said. "Now, your mother is a fine woman, but she couldn't abide a dog about the place. So you never got a chance to learn how smart a dog can be. When that dog is Lassie, it is pretty doggone smart!"

"I know," Paul said with heavy sarcasm. "One *woof* means 'left.' Two *bowwows* is 'right.' And an *arf* means 'Stop, you dolt, you're about to hit a tree!' "

"Don't try to be funny," Sam said. "Do you want to take the shovels out or don't you?"

"Let's go!" Paul said quickly.

The three—Paul, Sam, and Lassie—went out to the baggageman's pickup truck. They quickly loaded twenty-five shovels from the section hands' tool crib.

Paul and Lassie climbed into the cab. "I hope this old wreck will be able to make it," Paul said.

The pickup had been rebuilt from some sort of army surplus, and it resembled a junk pile on wheels.

"She may not look like much," Sam said

loyally, "but old Lizzie has the heart of a mountain goat. They don't make 'em like her anymore."

"No wonder," Paul retorted. "She must be as old as that old burro of Hardrock's. Say, is Comstock still alive?"

"That package of cussedness is like Wild Mountain Creek," Sam replied. "She may sort of dry up in the winter, but she's back kicking up her heels in the spring."

The mention of the burro, Comstock, brought Paul's mind back to Hardrock Hartley and the mystery of his condition.

"Sam," he asked, "what is wrong with Hardrock?"

The baggageman dropped his head, swallowing hard. "I guess you have to know," he said in a low voice. "But I can't talk about it. Somebody else will have to tell you. It hurts me too much."

"I see," Paul said, his own hurt nearly choking him. He was sure now that his guess had been right. Hardrock had probably been crippled in his fall from Wild Mountain.

"No, you're wrong!" Sam burst out. "It's worse than you think!"

"But I didn't say what I thought!" Paul protested.

"Whatever you thought, it's worse than that!" Sam insisted, the hurt in his eyes troubling Paul even more than the words themselves.

Paul jumped slightly as something wet and cold touched his hand. He looked down to see Lassie's nose rubbing against him. She whined, and her intelligent brown eyes looked up sadly at the boy.

"She acts almost human," Paul said to Sam. "She's sad when we're sad and laughs when we laugh."

"That dog has more sense than both of us put together," Sam replied, struggling to dismiss his unhappy mood. "But you had better get moving. Corey Stuart needs those shovels."

"So long, Sam," Paul said. "Will you tell my mother where I am?"

As he drove away, Paul hoped fervently that his guess about Hardrock Hartley was wrong. To be strapped in a chair the rest of his life would be a sentence of doom to a man like Hardrock. He was the kind who had to be moving all the time.

But soon Paul was lost in the welcome renewal of his old friendship with the trees of the forest. What he was driving through now was primarily a pine belt, although Douglas fir, incense cedar, and white fir could be seen among the irregularly barked ponderosa pines.

As the road wound upward he started to see more and more sugar pines, true monarchs of trees, towering above all the other pines. Then the road broke out into the open for the first time, and he could see down into a valley far below. In two places the thick pine stands were broken by meadows where cattle grazed. Beyond, stark, naked rock towered up like great granite teeth biting at the deep-blue sky.

To the north the smoke hiding the bare rocks above timberline was starting to clear away. This sign that the fire was now under control made Paul feel better.

The joy of the drive ended when Paul turned off the main road. He cut along a firebreak lane through an area devastated by forest fires. It had been reseeded, but it would not be anything but a desolate area for many years.

For more than a quarter of an hour the pickup bounced and slid and bucked over a twisting road that was nothing but a strip bulldozed through underbrush among the trees. Paul's arms ached from the struggle with the wheel, which was nearly jerked from his hands each time the pickup hit a hole.

"Whew!" Paul said to Lassie. "This is the hardest work I ever did!"

Shortly they were back in the timber and soon came to a place where the road radiated. This section of the national forest was new to

Paul, but he was sure of his direction. He turned north. Instantly Lassie barked sharply.

Paul looked around at her. "What's the matter with you?" he asked.

In answer the collie scrambled through the open window of the car's cab. She ran back a few steps, then stopped and looked around at Paul. He had jammed on the brakes when she left the pickup. It was plain she wanted him to go the other way.

"Look," he said, cross and tired, "you are dead wrong. The fire camp is north. Get in here!"

Lassie barked again and trotted away, looking back over her shoulder at the angry driver.

Paul's patience had worn thin. "You can play games if you want to," he said, "but I've got to get these shovels to Mr. Stuart. You can just walk!"

He started the pickup. Lassie barked, but Paul ignored her warning. She stopped and sadly trotted after the pickup. Paul stopped the truck and opened the cab door for her to get in. But Lassie turned and started back again.

"You are as stubborn as Hardrock's Comstock!" he cried.

He let out the clutch and the pickup started jerkily. Lassie began to follow. Paul felt a little better. Angry as he was at the dog, he did not want to lose her. He drove slowly and kept looking into the rearview mirror to see if she was following.

This brief inattention made him slow to see the danger ahead. The road had turned down along the rim of the national forest. Here it suddenly disappeared under masses of eroded sand and hardened mud.

Poor conservation in the area beyond the national forest had stripped away timber in the watershed. Slashing mountain rains had done the rest.

In a sickening flash Paul realized what had happened. He had been right about this turn being the shortest way to the fire camp. But

Lassie had known the way was blocked and that they had to circle around in what appeared to be the wrong direction.

Paul frantically jammed on the brakes. The wheels locked. The pickup lurched into a skid. The back wheels went over the edge of the embankment.

Paul tried to jump, but he couldn't get the cab door open in time. As the truck turned over, he jammed his feet hard against the floorboard and gripped the wheel in a desperate attempt to brace himself for the coming crash.

"Oh, why didn't I listen to Lassie!" he thought as the pickup rolled over.

2   The Tragedy of Hardrock

THE WORLD whirled dizzily for the boy trapped in the cab of the overturning pickup. He was thrown heavily against the top, but his desperate grip on the steering wheel kept him from being knocked unconscious.

The vehicle hit on its side in the loose sand and slid to a crashing halt in a stand of pines. A lodgepole pine, its roots loosened by the erosion, crashed across the cab. The pickup swerved around, the back end crushing a young incense cedar, and there it stopped.

Paul coughed, stifled by the blinding cloud of dust that fogged into the cab. He tried to pull himself up, but he found he couldn't move his left arm.

For one frightened moment he thought his arm was broken, but it was only numbed by the hard blow when he struck the top of the cab as the pickup turned over. Some life was already coming back into it. And with the restored movement came an awful ache.

Sweat rolled down the trapped boy's face, plowing muddy furrows through the layer of dust. Painfully Paul twisted himself free of the steering wheel. He looked around for a way to crawl out.

Some of the dust had settled. For the first time he could get a halfway clear view of his position. It filled him with dismay. The cab door on the driver's side was pressed against the loose gravel at the foot of the embankment. The opposite door was blocked by the lodgepole pine that had crashed across it. Dirt had cascaded against the windshield, so there was no chance to break it and get out that way. The glass was already cracked by the weight of the stones in the gravel, and there was a genuine danger that Paul would be engulfed by the dirt if it gave way.

The back window of the metal cab was too small for him to crawl through. Also, it was blocked by the thick foliage of the incense cedar. The strong perfume that gives the tree its name rose from the crushed leaves and filled the cab.

"What will I do?" Paul wondered. He had a fearful vision of himself starving to death in his crumpled metal prison.

Then he heard Lassie's anxious bark. It was the most beautiful sound he had ever heard in his life.

"Lassie!" he cried. "Here I am, Lassie! Go get help! Go get Mr. Stuart, Lassie!"

He heard the dog whine. From the sound of her movements she seemed to be circling.

"Lassie!" he cried more anxiously. "Lassie, please go get Mr. Stuart! Corey Stuart, Lassie!"

Still the collie did not go. Paul's anxiety gave way to anger.

"I thought Sam said you were smart!" he cried. "You are the dumbest dog I ever saw! Go get Stuart! Go! Go! *Go!*"

Lassie ignored the angry command. In Paul's anger and near panic it did not occur to him that Lassie had been right before and might be right again.

He tried to straighten his stiff, aching legs. Then he pushed against the scaly bark of the lodgepole pine blocking the cab door.

It was solidly wedged, and all he did was scratch the palms of his hands. He gave up, dividing his resentment between the dog who would not obey his command and the tree that blocked his way.

Paul had long admired this tree, and now for it to block his way seemed almost like betrayal by an old friend.

Hardrock Hartley had been the first to tell him the story of the lodgepole pine. The tree had been a favorite of the old prospector. He claimed it had more character than any other

tree in the forest. Hardrock had told Paul that
Captain Meriwether Lewis of the Lewis and
Clark expedition had named the tree after seeing Indians travel hundreds of miles to get it
to build tepees.

Now the boy tried to think, but a headache
from the bump he had received made it difficult. What was the lesson Hardrock had drilled
into him so many times? "You are never licked,
son, until *you* admit it."

"Well," Paul told himself grimly, "I'm not
admitting it yet!"

Then from outside he heard a noise that
made him sit up. It was the scratch of paws
digging in the earth.

"Hey!" he cried in astonishment. "She's trying to dig me out!"

His heart began to pound with renewed hope.
He cried out to the collie, "Lassie! Lassie! Keep
it up, girl!"

He listened, trying to place the position
where she was digging. He decided that it was

behind the windshield where dirt had packed against the cracked glass.

He started kicking against the glass with his shoe heel. He hoped to help her by digging at the dirt from his side. He realized his mistake when the glass gave way. The dirt poured into the cab. There was no way he could escape it. Dust boiled around him again, and in seconds he was buried up to his waist.

Dirt kept pouring in, but at a slower rate, as Lassie dug deeper into the mass blocking his escape.

Paul was trapped, a prisoner, until Lassie could get a way cleared to the windshield.

Finally, with Paul pushing from inside and Lassie digging on the slope, the boy was able to force his way through the narrow opening.

He threw his arms about the collie's neck and hugged her close to him.

"Sam was right!" he cried. "You are everything Sam said about you! I'll never argue with you again!"

There were other things he wanted to say, but he could not put them into words. He could only say, "Lassie! Lassie!"

The collie seemed to understand. She put her beautiful head on the boy's knee and whined softly.

They were sitting like this, with Paul worrying about how he would explain the wreck to Sam Gresham, when Lassie suddenly raised her head. Her tulip ears twitched. She barked —but it was not an unfriendly bark. Then she started scrambling up the embankment.

Paul could see nothing. He stood up, wincing as bruises and strained muscles protested his movements. The top of the embankment cut off his view, and he still could not see what had attracted Lassie's attention.

Then he heard a boy's voice. "Lassie! Hey there, girl! What happened? I saw a truck go off the embankment. Who's in it?"

Although he still could not see the speaker, Paul recognized the voice.

"Tom!" he called. "Tom Toomey! Here I am, Tom. Down here!"

Seconds later Tom Toomey and Lassie appeared at the top of the roadbed.

"Paul!" he cried, surprised. "What happened?"

Sheepishly Paul told Tom how he had ignored Lassie's warning.

"Sam is going to be angry," Paul said ruefully. "He loves this wreck the way Hardrock loves that burro, Comstock."

A shadow passed over Tom Toomey's face at the mention of the old prospector. Paul was quick to note it.

"Tom," he said quickly, "what is the trouble with Hardrock? Sam wouldn't tell me."

"I guess he wouldn't," the other boy said. "Sam was real broken up about it. You know he and Hardrock have been friends practically forever."

"But what is it?" Paul asked impatiently.

"He's crazy!" Tom blurted out.

"Crazy? No! I don't believe it. Not Hard-rock."

"I'm afraid it's true, Paul," Tom said. "I know how much you think of Hardrock. He's been just like a father to you."

Paul closed his eyes and shivered. This tragic news was difficult to believe, but he had known Tom Toomey all his life. He knew that the other boy would never lie to him.

Suddenly he felt too sick and shaken to stand. He sat down heavily on the edge of the overturned pick-up.

"Yes," he said in a low, choked voice, "when my father died Hardrock took over. But he was more than a father. He— Oh, I can't put it in words, Tom."

Paul looked miserably out across the scarred, eroded land beyond the border of the national forest. At that moment his spirits were as badly torn up as the land.

In his early childhood, Paul, his body rav-aged by serious illnesses, had been smaller and weaker than other boys his age. His inability to keep up with them had affected him deeply. Hardrock, a small man himself, had understood how Paul felt and had gone out of his way to give Paul courage. He made the boy understand, through his own examples, that physical size is the least of the things necessary to be a real man.

As he had grown into his teens, Paul had begun to fill out and had overcome his early weakness. But he never forgot the lesson Hardrock taught him. The passing years had not lessened his gratitude to the old prospector but had only strengthened it.

Paul took a deep breath, fighting down the grief that threatened to choke him. When he could speak he asked, "How did it happen, Tom?"

"He was up on Wild Mountain prospecting," Tom said. "Somehow he fell off a ledge. He crushed in the top of his skull. Dad and I found him there."

"And the wound left him—" Paul choked, unable to say the word.

"We took him to Black Rock. He regained consciousness, but he didn't know any of us. He seemed to remember his younger days, but he couldn't understand where he was or who we were. He seemed to think we were a bunch of crooks who had captured him."

"I know what that means," Paul said. "When he was about eighteen a crooked sheriff up in the Mother Lode country robbed a bank. To cover himself, he tried to blame it on Hardrock. There was a big chase and a fight before Hardrock cleared himself."

"That must be it," Tom said. "He kept shouting that we weren't going to hang him for something he didn't do."

"That figures," Paul said. "A teller was killed in the robbery, and Hardrock was charged with murder."

"Well, he sure believes he's back in that scrape," Tom said. "He was like a wildcat. He broke loose and got away. Dr. Samuels said there is a piece of bone pressing on his brain. If something isn't done about it, he'll probably—" Tom choked on the word "die."

"That's terrible!" Paul said shakily. "Where is he?"

"Nobody knows," Tom said. "He's either in the forest or on Wild Mountain or in the desert. We looked for him. We couldn't even find a track."

"We've got to find him somehow!" Paul said. "We can't leave him out there to die alone."

"He could be anywhere," Tom said.

Paul took a deep breath. He knew his friend was right. At the northern corner of the forest lands there jutted up a monstrously rough area of rocks clustered about Wild Mountain. It was an area that lived up to its name. Above the timberline it was a barren place of broken ridges and sheer cliffs. Wild Mountain marked the border between the forest and neighboring ranchland on one side and barren desert on the other. Its slopes were the scenes of almost constant, vicious storms.

Paul remembered Hardrock telling him this was the cause of the desert valley on the other side of the mountain. Air conditions in and about Wild Mountain caused all clouds moving in from the coast to empty their water on the mountain, causing the barrenness in the valley beyond.

"Unless you knew exactly where he was heading," Tom said, "the chance of finding him is one in a million. Dad says he's a goner."

Paul thought of what Hardrock had said so often: "You're not beaten until you admit it to yourself."

He looked at Tom. His friend's face was grim and drawn.

"We can find him, Tom. You and I," he said.

"Do you know where he might have gone?" Tom asked, his face brightening.

"Maybe," Paul said slowly.

"Okay, then," Tom said eagerly. "We'll get

Corey Stuart to let Lassie come with us. You haven't met Corey, have you, Paul? He's one swell guy."

"I guess we had better get moving," Paul replied. "I've got to get to the advanced fire camp and let Mr. Stuart know what happened. Maybe he has a jeep or something he can send back for the shovels I was bringing him."

"The camp is over the ridge," Tom said. "I was just coming back from there when I saw you go off the road. I had gone over to volunteer to help the fire crews. But they have the fire out now."

The two boys, with Lassie running ahead, started through the forest, following the trail Tom had taken from the fire camp. Paul still ached from the accident, and each step was agony for him. However, he gritted his teeth and trudged along after Tom for half an hour or so. Then the worst of the climb was over. Soon the two boys came to the road leading in to the fire camp.

Here the wind changed, and for the first time
Paul caught the smell of smoke in the air. Shortly after that, they came to the base fire camp.

It was a sleepy-looking place, for the day
crews were out on the fire line "mopping up"
and killing pockets of fire. The night crews
were asleep under a stretched tarpaulin. Only
a few men were in sight. Two mechanics were
working on a truck, and two other men were
overhauling a portable water pump.

The sight was familiar to Paul. He had been
too young to work on the fire line before he left
for school, but twice during big blazes he had
assisted the former district ranger by working
on the "status map" at the headquarters tent.

Nothing had changed. A fire camp was a fire
camp. There was the same blackboard erected
in front of the headquarters tent—the status
map he used to keep up.

But now a tall man in a Forest Service uniform came out of the tent. He carried the
familiar clipboard in his hand and started

marking in chalk the latest reports of fire conditions. The information showed not only where pockets of fire still burned, but also the position of the different crews. By looking at the status board, the fire boss could tell at a glance exactly what was going on.

"Hi, Hank!" Tom called to the tall, sandy-haired man at the board.

"Oh, hello, Tom," the ranger said in a soft Arkansas drawl. "You made a pretty fast trip home."

"Well, I didn't get there," Tom said. "This is Paul Carter. He's the son of Mrs. Ruth Carter. She has the ranch adjoining ours. He's been away to school."

"Well, I'm mighty proud to meet you, Paul," the ranger said. "I'm Hank Whitfield, Corey Stuart's assistant. You look sort of banged up. They treat you rough back there in the wilds of the big city?"

"No," Paul said with a grin, warming instantly to the friendly Arkansan. "I'm afraid I got into trouble because I didn't listen to Lassie. She tried to tell me the way to go, and I wouldn't listen."

"Same thing happened to me," Hank said with a rueful grin. "Finally I admitted that she's smarter than I am. Since then I've had no trouble."

"The next time she says *arf* to me, I intend to say, 'Yes, ma'am!' " Paul replied.

"I know how you feel," Hank said. "Paul Carter—hmmm. Name sounds familiar. Oh, I know! You're the one Corey said was bringing the shovels out from Black Rock."

"Only I didn't," Paul said. "I had a wreck."

Then he told Hank Whitfield what had happened. He was relieved when the tall ranger took the loss calmly.

"We'll get someone to take the jeep out and pick up the shovels," he said. "Our mop-up crews need them pretty badly. We'll also see about pulling out Sam's pickup. I doubt if it's hurt much. It's a wreck anyway."

"Is there any way Paul can get home from here?" Tom asked.

"Well, he can—"

Hank paused as a jeep loaded with men turned into the camp from the main road.

"Hey!" Tom said. "There's Dad in the jeep. He can take Paul with us. I wonder what he came for."

"Hmmmm," Hank said thoughtfully. "He doesn't look very happy."

"Say," Tom said uneasily, "he does look disturbed. That's not like him at all."

"No, it isn't," Hank agreed. "Come on! Let's see what new trouble he's bringing us."

3   Trouble with Tom

THE JEEP pulled into the camp parking lot. Whitfield, followed by the two boys and Lassie, headed toward it. Several men climbed out of the car.

Fred Ross Toomey passed a hasty greeting to his son and to Paul. Then he said to Whitfield, "Another fire broke out just above Horace Ball's wheat, Hank."

"I'll get a crew out," Whitfield said quickly.

"We were able to take care of it ourselves. It had just got a start," Tom's father said. "That wasn't what we came for, Hank. We want to head off any more fires."

There was a bleak, unhappy expression on Fred Toomey's face. Paul remembered him as a good-natured man who seemed to take everything in life with a grin. It made Paul uneasy to see Mr. Toomey like this.

"You sound as if you know what is causing the fires," Whitfield said, looking keenly at Tom's father.

"Yes, I guess we do. Don't you think so, boys?" Fred Toomey looked around at the four men who had come with him.

"You think there's a firebug?" Hank asked.

"We're positive," Mr. Toomey replied.

"This surprises me," Hank returned. "There has been a lot of lightning lately. Corey and I figured it caused the blazes."

"No," Mr. Toomey said. "It was Hardrock Hartley!"

"No!" Paul cried. "I don't believe it! Not Hardrock! Why, he was one of the first men in this area to preach conservation! He would be the last person in the world to start a fire!"

"I know," Mr. Toomey said. "He was also the first one to bring up the idea of creating a national forest here. He—"

"Then how can you accuse him of being a firebug?" Paul cried.

"He's not himself, Paul," Fred Toomey said impatiently. "You don't understand the condition he is in. I'm not saying the old man is doing it deliberately. He doesn't know. . . ."

"Not Hardrock," Paul replied with a definite shake of his head.

"I know what you think of the old man, Paul," Fred Toomey said, his voice a mixture of sympathy and irritation. "But you are popping off now without knowing what you are talking about. Have you seen Hartley since his accident?"

"No, I haven't," Paul admitted. "But—"

"But you are talking with your heart instead of your head!" Mr. Toomey snapped. "Why don't you be quiet until you know what you're talking about?"

Tom's father turned to Hank Whitfield, leaving Paul red-faced with embarrassment. He could tell from the other men's faces that they agreed with Mr. Toomey.

"This last blaze was right where it would have spread into our wheat and grass," Toomey said to Whitfield. "I'm not claiming the old man did it deliberately, Hank. I think he started cooking fires and in his addled condition failed to put out the embers."

"That's what the rest of us think, too, Whitfield," one of the other men said. The rest nodded in agreement.

Paul looked at them in dismay. "I know Hardrock didn't do anything like that," he cried. "You don't know how he preached fire discipline to me for years. He once told me fire was the one thing he was afraid of in this world."

"Well, I admire your loyalty to your friend," Fred Toomey said. His square, weather-beaten face wore a more kindly expression than it had a moment ago. "But you should realize what it would have meant if fire had jumped across to our ranches. It would have ruined us all—your mother included."

"Yes, but—" Paul began.

"Let me finish, please," Mr. Toomey said sharply. "What uncontrolled fire would do to the national forest would be just as disastrous as its effects on the ranches. You should know how long it takes to replace burned-over timber. And that doesn't begin to consider the damage caused by erosion of the ruined watershed. The—"

He stopped and grinned sheepishly. "I'm beginning to talk like Corey Stuart now."

The other men laughed, remembering how Fred Toomey had been one of those who had originally fought conservation until Hardrock Hartley's persuasiveness and a nearly disastrous flood had made him as ardent a conservationist as any forest ranger.

"You really think Hardrock accidently set these fires?" Hank Whitfield asked.

"Yes, and we must find him," Mr. Toomey

said. He looked at Paul's white, tense face. "We must find him for his own good. The man is in terrible condition. He'll die if he isn't taken back to the hospital."

"I thought the sheriff had a posse out looking for him," Hank said.

"They don't seem to be doing any good," Mr. Toomey said. "We want Corey Stuart to send his fire crews out as soon as he can spare them."

"I'm sure Corey will agree to that," Hank said. "He— Hey! Here he comes now. I see his station wagon pulling up."

Paul followed the group over to the parking area where the station wagon had stopped. His spirits were lower than they had ever been before in his entire life.

"They'll kill him, without meaning to, if they run him down!" he whispered to himself.

Tom Toomey, walking along beside him, gave his friend a sharp look, but did not say anything.

The man getting out of the station wagon was tall and well built. The forest ranger uniform with its big Stetson hat seemed part of the man himself. His friendly, yet strong face appealed to Paul, who found himself liking the man at first sight.

"What's the trouble?" Corey Stuart asked when he saw the group coming toward him. Then he added with mock dismay, "What have I done wrong now?"

Fred Toomey laughed. "What you've done is boss just about the best and quickest job I've ever seen of putting out what could have been a disastrous fire. That's what you've done!"

"And what you've done is stretch the truth just about as far as it will go without breaking completely," Corey Stuart said with a smile.

"No," Mr. Toomey replied with a grin nearly as wide as Corey Stuart's. "I'm not claiming I'm always truthful, but this time I'm right on the mark. That fire was pretty close to the edge of the national forest lands. If it had gotten out

of hand, every one of us here would be ruined."

"Corey," Hank put in, "Fred reported another blaze. He and Weaver and Booth got it out before it had a good start."

Stuart's grin turned to concern. "That makes three fires in three days," he said.

"That's what we came to see you about, Corey," Mr. Toomey said. "We think Hardrock Hartley set those fires."

"That's hard to believe," Corey Stuart answered, his face showing his concern.

"I don't mean he is doing it intentionally," Mr. Toomey said. "He doesn't know what he is doing. You remember how he acted at the hospital? He's crazy, Corey. Just plain crazy."

"Do you have any proof?" Corey Stuart asked.

"We found his burro's hoofprints just above the place where the last fire started," Fred Toomey said. "That's why we think he came back into the forest."

"Yes," one of the other men put in. "The

sheriff's men thought he must have headed back for his ranch. They went searching in that direction. One of them came back to my place this morning for supplies. They haven't found him. This must be the reason."

"Mr. Stuart!" Paul cried. "I *know* Hardrock didn't leave any carelessly killed campfires. You see, he—"

"I told you, Paul, that too much is at stake to depend on our hearts instead of our heads," Fred Toomey said severely. He turned to Corey Stuart. "Paul and Hardrock were pretty close before the boy went off to school," he explained.

"Regardless of whether the old man accidentally set the fires or not," Corey said, "we must find him. I thought the sheriff's men were taking care of the search. But if he is in the forest, we must find him for his own good."

"That's right," Fred Toomey said, looking at Paul with a little less irritation. "We're not trying to be mean to the old man. I like Hardrock as well as anybody here. What we want to do, Corey, is take all the fire crews and send them out just as quickly as they finish mopping up."

"That we can do," Corey said quickly. "We'll comb every square inch of the forest until we find him."

"But don't you see?" Paul cried. "That is just what you can't do!"

"Oh, for goodness' sake, Paul!" Fred Toomey said in disgust.

Lassie looked from the angry, fearful boy to the annoyed man. She whined softly, disturbed by their disagreement.

"Wait a minute, Fred," Corey Stuart said. "Let's see what Paul has to say. Just why shouldn't we search for Hardrock, Paul? His life is at stake, the way I see it."

Paul warmed to Corey Stuart's willingness to listen to him instead of brusquely overriding his opinion as the others had done.

"Mr. Stuart, I know Hardrock better than anybody. From the time I was two years old we were together every day until I left for school. Tom Toomey told me what happened at the hospital. The injury to his head has made him forget all that has happened in the last forty years, and he thinks he's back being pursued by that crooked sheriff who tried to hang him so long ago."

"Yes, I heard about that," the ranger said.

"Don't you see then?" Paul cried earnestly. "Thinking that, he isn't going to let himself be taken alive. You'll never capture him. You'll have to kill him or somebody else will be killed. Hardrock thinks he's fighting for his life, Mr. Stuart! If you knew him like I do, you'd know he never gives up."

"I understand," Corey Stuart said quietly. "I think all of us understand. It's a risk we must take. The risk to ourselves and the risk to Hardrock. This man is hurt. He doesn't know what he's doing. He's a menace to himself and to others, Paul."

"That's right," Tom's father said quickly.

"Get the idea out of your head, Paul, that we're doing something cruel to the old man. This is not only the sensible thing to do. It is the human thing as well."

"Yes," Mr. Stuart agreed. "If he is inside the national forest, it is my responsibility to find him."

"I know he has to be found," Paul said, his voice tense with his eagerness to make Corey Stuart believe him. "But if a group goes looking for him, all he'll do is back up against the wall and fight until he kills himself. But I can find him. He'll listen to me, Mr. Stuart. I know I can talk him into coming back to the hospital."

"I wonder if you could," Corey Stuart mused softly.

"Not a chance of it, Corey," Tom's father said with a positive shake of his head.

"No," one of the other men said. "Every one of us has known Hardrock longer than you have, Paul. I've known him for forty-five years. Yet he didn't recognize me."

"He came charging out of that hospital yelling that we weren't going to hang him for something he didn't do," Fred Toomey said. "He was so excited that no one could have stopped him. You would have had to have been there to believe it. That blow has set Hardrock's mind back forty years. If he didn't recognize any of us and thought we were all his enemies, he'll do the same to you."

"In his condition he's as dangerous as a rattlesnake," the other man added.

"Worse," Mr. Toomey said positively. "He won't rattle a warning before he strikes. Any one person would be foolish to try and find him alone. No, Paul. We appreciate how you feel, but it is impossible."

"But, Mr. Stuart!" Paul cried. "I know—"

"I'm sorry, Paul," Corey Stuart said kindly but firmly in a tone of voice that told the desperate boy that nothing would change the ranger's mind.

"Perhaps you *could* succeed," Stuart went

on. "But we can't take a chance. There is too much at stake. This man is sick and injured. There is absolutely no way of knowing what he will do."

Paul swallowed hard. He did not reply, but his mind was working furiously as he tried to think of some argument that would convince them that he could succeed even though all of the others might fail.

He remembered vividly the tales Hardrock Hartley had told him about that bitter pursuit forty years ago. A dozen times the innocent man had been trapped by his pursuers, and each time he had fought his way to freedom simply because he would not give up.

Today, Paul felt sure, Hardrock was every bit as fierce in his determination to win at all costs, but the tremendous strength of his youth had been sapped by age. This was something the old prospector would never admit. If he tried to climb sheer cliffs, swing across chasms on hastily stretched ropes, leap from trees onto his pursuers, or shoot it out with them in the darkness of a mine shaft, it would be his death.

Then there was the awful chance that the pursuit would turn the old man, with his injured brain, into a murderer. In his desperate flight—certain that his pursuers were trying to kill him—the old prospector would probably try to kill his enemies before they killed him.

Yet Paul realized it was useless to try anymore to make these men understand this. It was true all of them had known Hardrock Hartley even before Paul was born. But had they known him as well? Had Hardrock ever poured out his secret dreams and ambitions to them as he had to Paul? They would have laughed at his wild schemes, but the boy had listened with wonder—and had believed.

"A man's bound to win if he just keeps fighting. Never give up, Paul. Doggone it, boy, keep going!"

Paul could close his eyes and see the granite look on Hardrock's face when he said those words, repeated dozens of times over the years of their association.

"And that is what I'm going to do!" Paul told himself grimly. "I'm going to keep on fighting —for Hardrock's life!"

"I suggest we go over to the place where you found the burro's tracks and start from there," Corey Stuart said to Mr. Toomey.

"That's what we had in mind, Corey," Mr. Toomey said. "The trail disappears on some rocky ground, but we hoped that Lassie could pick up the scent."

"Let's hope that she can," the ranger said. "I can get away now, with the fire well under control. I'll go with you. Hank can send along some of the fire crews when they finish mopping up."

"Good," Mr. Toomey said. Then he added to Paul, "Would you like to come along with us? You can call your mother on Corey's phone so she won't be worried when you don't come home."

"No, thank you," Paul said shortly.

Fred Toomey opened his mouth to reply but thought better of it. He gave Paul a keen look.

One of the other men put into words what Toomey was thinking. "You wouldn't be intending to shortcut us and try to get to Hardrock first, would you?" the man asked.

Paul flushed. "How would I know where he is?" he asked somewhat sullenly. "I just got back."

The man, Jess Turner, grinned. "You gave away your hand, Paul, when you said you didn't want to go along. I know *you*, young man. You don't give up easy."

"I just don't want to go," Paul said hurriedly. "Excuse me, please."

He turned away hastily. Tom Toomey looked after him uncertainly, then followed his friend.

"Paul!" Tom called, his face creased with worry.

Paul stopped, waiting for his friend to join him. Tom looked back to make sure that they were out of earshot of the others.

"You aren't really going to try and find Hardrock by yourself?"

Paul looked at him suspiciously. "What do you care?" he asked.

"Paul, Dad is right," Tom said earnestly. "I was there in the hospital. He's crazy, Paul. He doesn't know what he's doing. He thinks everyone is against him. Remember, I've known him as long as you have. He called me a 'bushwhacking rascal' and tried to brain me with a water pitcher."

"You weren't as close to him as I was," Paul replied. "I *know* he won't hurt me, Tom."

"You can't do it, Paul! If Hardrock doesn't kill you, you'll drown! The recent rains on Wild Mountain have Wild Creek on a rampage. You can't get across like we used to."

"Who said I was going that way?" Paul asked uneasily.

"That's where you think he went," Tom said accusingly. "I remember how Hardrock used to take us over to that old Indian cave just the same as you do."

Paul flushed with uneasy anger. He grabbed Tom by the arm.

"If you tell anybody about that place, I'll—"

Tom jerked free. "You'll what?" he snapped. "If you try to threaten me, I'll knock your block off!"

"Look, that cave was Hardrock's secret! Nobody ever knew about it except you and me! If you go and tell your father Hardrock is up there, I'll—"

Paul left the rest unfinished, but his doubled fists left no doubt what he meant.

"Ever since you got back you've been trying to act like a big shot!" Tom cried. "Well, you don't impress me one bit. You—"

"Hey! What are you boys doing?" It was the sharp voice of Tom's father. He came walking rapidly toward them. "I've got enough worries without you two adding to them. I won't put up with any fights."

"We aren't fighting," Tom said quickly.

Paul said nothing. He stared bitterly to the north where tree-covered mountains blended into the blue haze of the horizon.

"Somewhere out there," he thought with a lump in his throat, "the man I think most of in this world is going to die if I don't find a way to help him."

Fred Toomey looked from his son to Paul. There was deep concern on his face. Although he was a brusque man who all too often failed to consider anyone's opinions but his own, he was at heart a good man. His regard for Paul was almost as deep as for his own son. It hurt him to see the two boys quarreling. Like so many of his kind, he was unable to put his emotions into words and often hid his concern behind a show of anger.

Corey Stuart, observing Paul's manner, was quick to interrupt. "Oh, friends wouldn't be friends if they didn't have a few words now and then," he said quickly. "But let's leave fighting for tomorrow—if tomorrow ever comes! Right now, we have work to do."

He turned and asked Hank Whitfield to bring up the Forest Service station wagon. Toomey and the men who had come with him would go back in the jeep that brought them. Corey would take the rest with him.

"And I'd like you to go with us, Paul," he said to the angry, worried boy.

"I don't—" Paul began and then hesitated.

He realized that since Tom had guessed the possible secret of Hardrock's hiding place, he could not hope to get there on foot before the others arrived by vehicle. He decided it was best to go with the men and try to do what little he could.

"If they would just let me go in alone!" he thought, but he knew that men of strong opinion like Fred Toomey and the others would never listen to any advice from him.

Paul shot a quick glance at Tom.

"It's all his fault," he thought. And he felt

that a lifetime friendship was in danger of ending.

Suddenly through his bitterness and anger he felt a sharp pang. His and Tom's had been a wonderful friendship. It hurt to have this happen.

4   The Lost Trail

THE BURRO tracks which Fred Toomey thought were the clue to the missing man's whereabouts were at the limits of the national forest. Here the trees gave way to grasslands as the ground fell sharply.

They followed the tracks past the burned-out area where the men had earlier fought the fire Mr. Toomey blamed on Hardrock Hartley. The trail curved back into the forest, but soon disappeared into a rocky area that swept down to Wild Creek.

"This is the end of it," Fred Toomey said. "Unless Lassie can pick up the trail, we haven't much hope."

The men stooped to inspect the tracks. "The

tracks are pretty fresh," one said. "You notice
the dragging and the shape of the depression?
Comstock was running when he made these."

"Frightened by the fire," Toomey replied.
"The way I figure it, Hardrock tried to camp
here with the burro. In his confused state of
mind he let his campfire get out of control. The
fire was what attracted our attention."

Corey Stuart looked at the blackened area
where the men had extinguished the blaze.

"You did a wonderful job getting it out
before it spread," he said.

"It was luck," Mr. Toomey said, pleased by
the ranger's praise. "We had been over toward
Hardrock's ranch—if you can call that shack
in the desert a ranch. We'd been helping the
sheriff search for him."

"Yes," Phil Booth, another rancher, put in.
"We saw the smoke just as it started."

The ranger looked thoughtfully at the tracks.
"Let me see," he said. "It has been about
twenty-four hours since Hartley escaped from

the hospital. He could have walked this far by now. We had best fan out and see if we can pick up the trail."

They crossed the small stream and spread out to cover as much ground as possible. Paul went with them, hoping desperately that Lassie would not pick up the burro's scent again.

Soon the men were combing the thick growth of trees and brush. They went on for another half-hour. Twice Lassie picked up a scent and then lost it as a stream or rocky ground caused the trail to fade.

Paul realized with dismay that they were nearing the river known locally as Wild Creek. That meant that they were moving directly to the place he was sure Hardrock had gone—a small rocky point beside Wild Creek. Its granite base had withstood centuries of the river's wear. In its pine-choked slopes was a small cave decorated with Indian pictographs. The entrance was well-screened, for it had evidently been the secret retreat of Indian medicine men.

Hardrock had once taken Paul and Tom there to look around.

"The only thing I can do," Paul told himself, "is to get there ahead of the others. Then—if I can just make Hardrock understand. . . ."

He started to run, but very quickly he had to slow down. He had been away from the mountains for two years, and his lungs were not used to the thinner air. Gasping, he leaned against the irregularly scaled bark of a huge sugar pine and tried to get his breath. But only for a moment or so. He didn't want to waste any more time than he had to.

Then, taking it more slowly, he started again. The sugar pines were thinning out, and he could see the nearly upright branches on the tops of western white pines. He knew that he was approaching the eight-thousand-foot level. The sugar pine rarely grows beyond seventy-five hundred feet and the white pine rarely below eight thousand feet.

Paul moved on, hurrying as best he could. He

kept ahead of the others, but he did not gain much. Several times he heard Lassie barking. He thought with dismayed anxiety, "She's picked up the scent!"

He started to run again. To his right he heard Tom Toomey shout to his father, "Lassie has found something, Dad!"

Despite his labored breathing, Paul pushed on. Lassie stopped barking, but as he drew nearer, Paul could hear her whine. There were other sounds that he could not place. He still couldn't see what was happening, for some alpine willows blocked his view.

When he finally got close enough, he saw that Lassie had found the burro, Comstock. The little pack animal looked much older than Paul remembered her, but she had lost none of her stubbornness. The burro's feet were spread and solidly planted. She was pulling against the short length of frayed rope attached to her halter, resisting Lassie's determined tug at the other end.

Suddenly the collie, unable to budge the stubborn burro, dropped the rope from her teeth. She whirled around Comstock and nipped at the burro's heels to get her started.

Comstock kicked angrily, but Lassie jumped back. She nipped again. Then when the burro started to move into an awkward trot, Lassie darted around in front and seized the frayed halter rope with her teeth.

The smart little burro wasn't ready to give in yet. She trotted after Lassie's guiding pull for a few steps to allay the dog's suspicions. Then she suddenly jerked back. The rope slipped from Lassie's teeth. Comstock kicked her heels in the air with a youthfulness that belied her age and started for Wild Creek at a dead run.

Paul watched Lassie, a tawny streak, race after the determined burro. She caught the rope again. Comstock set her feet and again refused to be led.

In the background, Paul heard Tom Toomey

shout. It broke the spell that gripped him. For a moment he had been so interested in the struggle between dog and burro that he had forgotten the really important thing: Where was Hardrock Hartley?

He went on past them, hurrying toward Wild Creek. At this high elevation it was merely a stream, carrying a water flow only when rain cascaded from the barren granite cliffs of Wild Mountain towering up just north of this spot.

A depression in the rocks created a small pool near the point. Now, with no water coming down from the mountain's high slopes, the little pool was a perfect mirror. The rocky point and its western white pines made a beautiful reflection in the water. The mouth of the secret cave was still hidden, as Paul remembered it, by some alpine willows.

Paul stopped, bitterly disappointed. The outer shore of the pool, where he stood, was too rocky to retain footprints. But he could see the sand on the opposite side. It obviously had not been disturbed in any manner. While he could not see the cave-opening because of the willows, it was plain that Hardrock had not gone there as Paul thought he had.

Bewildered, Paul looked back to where Lassie was still struggling to lead the stubborn Comstock to Corey Stuart.

Paul watched the others arrive, but he did not go back himself. He didn't want to join them yet.

He heard Fred Toomey say, "Hardrock can't be far away. Comstock follows him around like a dog."

"Spread out," one of the other men said. "But watch yourselves. Remember, he doesn't know what he's doing. He's dangerous."

Circling around the men, Paul started back to the place where he had first seen Lassie and Comstock. He was thinking furiously.

"Maybe Comstock wasn't with Hardrock, after all," he told himself. "Maybe she was trying to find him the same as we were."

He remembered how Hardrock had always claimed that Comstock could trail a scent like a dog. He had never believed it. At times it delighted the old man to spin Bunyanesque yarns.

Then suddenly he remembered a time, five years ago, when he and Hardrock had left Comstock tied at the ranch because the burro had an injured foot. Comstock had chewed her rope in two and had followed them ten miles through the forest to a place where Hardrock was prospecting. She had never been there before, as he recalled it.

"Maybe she *was* trailing him," Paul thought. "Those were surely Hardrock's tracks back where we started today. He had to have been coming in this direction. He *had* to." Then a sudden thought struck him. "Unless—" he whispered in growing excitement. *"Unless. . . ."*

It had been so long since he had been in this area of Blue River National Forest that much had become hazy in his mind. Now, as he thought furiously, something buried deep in his mind began to tickle his memory.

"I'm sure," he said, gnawing his underlip in exasperation at not quite being able to recall that buried something. "I'm *sure* Hardrock and I came up this way one time when we didn't go to the cave. We went— Now, where was it?"

It made him both angry and worried that he couldn't remember. He knew that if Hardrock was as badly injured as Fred Toomey claimed, then any delays in finding the old man could result in Hardrock's death. The missing prospector had to be found and found quickly.

The rest of the searchers went forward, but Paul kept backtracking. He was seeking some landmark to spur his lagging memory rather than for tracks as the others were doing.

Then he found it!

He had come to an area where a forest fire had cut a wide slash through the stand of pines. Corey Stuart's crews had set out new saplings, but Paul knew that it would be twenty-five years or more before nature could completely make up for what a second's carelessness on the part of a hunter had caused.

As he stood for a moment resting and looking across the devastated area, dark clouds, which had been scuttling about the top of Wild Mountain, momentarily broke. The sun streaked through in a brilliant sunburst, highlighting the barren rocks and cliffs of the towering mountain. Part way up, a curious mixture of rock, shadow, and sunlight created the effect of a giant burro's head on the side of the mountain. It was slightly indistinct and could be seen from only one position.

Paul gasped as his memory came flooding back. That trick of rock and light had once been pointed out to him. He had been eight years old. Hardrock, wanting to inspect an old mine he had formerly owned high on the mountain, had brought Paul with him.

Now Paul remembered making the trip clinging to Comstock's back while Hardrock walked along beside them.

"We stopped just about here," Paul said, trying hard to recall what had happened on that day years before.

Then it came back to him with a rush. Almost fifty years ago Hardrock had tried to open a mine on Wild Mountain. The vein of gold was rich, but the mine had to be abandoned when the lower shafts flooded. Like the great mines of Tombstone, Arizona, it was impossible to pump the water out.

"I remember now," Paul said. "Hardrock wanted to see if the water still closed the mine."

It was a barren spot except for a few hardy whitebark pines growing in the cracks of the granite slab. As Paul now recalled, it had been a very difficult climb. Except for some alpine chipmunks who fed on the purplish, pitch-covered cones of the whitebark pines, it was likely that no one else had been there in more than forty years.

"*Oh!*" Paul gasped as something else hit him. "I remember now! This was the place where

Hardrock hid out when that crooked sheriff was trying to frame him!"

He was certain now that this was where Hardrock had gone. If in his confused mind he was reliving that long-ago adventure, it was natural for him to go back to the exact spot.

Paul looked back. In the distance he heard Comstock bray and Lassie bark. Urgent as it was for him to find Hardrock as quickly as possible, Paul was afraid the others would follow him if he left them. This he could not let happen. The terrible fight at the hospital was proof that Hardrock would fight to the death before he would let the others get near him.

Yet, if he wasn't brought back he would surely die from his head injuries. The doctor's report was that the broken piece of bone pressing on the injured man's brain would gradually work in deeper if not removed very soon.

He turned back reluctantly. The searching men moved together for a conference.

"I'm convinced now we made a mistake,"

Fred Toomey said. "I'm thinking now that Hardrock wasn't with Comstock. The burro is just wandering aimlessly around."

"Well, Fred, if he took the spur road from where we saw his tracks, he would have headed back toward his ranch," Phil Booth said.

"We just left there before we went for Corey," Toomey objected.

"He could have doubled back," Paul said quickly. "You would have missed him on the road when you went to the fire camp."

"That's right," Mr. Toomey said. He looked pleased, thinking that Paul had gotten over his idea of wanting to find the injured man himself.

But Tom Toomey knew Paul better than his father did. He looked suspiciously at the other boy. He knew that Paul never gave up. However, he said nothing. Neither of the boys had spoken to the other since their near-fight earlier.

"Well," Mr. Toomey said, "we'll go back to the ranch. Even if he's home, he needs help."

"If you're asking me," Booth said, "this craziness is nothing new. He's been crazy for years. You know what he told me last week? He claimed he had found a way to bring water into that desert valley."

"Yeah," Mr. Toomey said. "He told me the same thing. He said he was going to do for Desert Valley the same thing those promoters did when irrigation turned the Colorado Desert into Imperial Valley."

"I asked him where he would get the water," Booth said. "He just chuckled slyly. I should have realized then that he was off his rocker and notified the sheriff."

"I'll never believe that Hardrock was crazy before the accident," Paul said quickly. "If he said he could get water into the valley, I believe he had some scheme to do it."

"How?" Booth asked. "Okay, smart aleck, how?"

Paul's face reddened. Once again his loyalty to his old friend had trapped him. He could think of no way to get water into the barren valley. Over the years several reclamation engineers had inspected it. All had said it was impossible to do.

The arid section led off the lee side of Wild Mountain. The towering height of the famous landmark created weather conditions that brought almost constant clouds to the summit. This caused rain clouds to empty on the west side of Wild Mountain. None of the rain got into the adjoining dry valley. Irrigation proved impossible, for tunneling through the almost pure granite for that distance would cost too much money.

All this went through Paul's mind as he stood, silent. He had no answer.

Fred Toomey turned to Corey Stuart. "Can you come with us?"

"No," the ranger said. "I must check up on the fire mop-up crews before I can come. After that, I'll join you if you need me."

"I don't think we will," Mr. Toomey said.

"If Hardrock isn't in the forest, we won't need such a large searching party. There aren't many places outside where he can hide." He turned to Paul. "We can find room to take you along," he said.

For a moment Paul could not think of a good excuse for not going with them. He knew that he had to give one or they would suspect that he intended to get ahead of them in their search. But his mind was a blank. He could think of no excuse. Then Lassie helped him.

She had been lying beside Corey Stuart, her long muzzle resting on her outstretched paws. Now she jumped up suddenly. Unnoticed by the others, Comstock was moving quietly away. Lassie grabbed the piece of halter rope. The grizzled old burro brayed indignantly.

"Oh!" Paul said quickly. "I'd like to go, but you don't need me. Comstock does. I guess I can help Hardrock more by taking care of his old friend. I'll lead her back."

"Neither you nor anybody else can lead that

skinful of balkiness anywhere unless she has a mind to go," Fred Toomey said. "But you are welcome to try."

"I'll stay and help you," Tom said quickly.

"I don't need any help, thank you," Paul replied even more quickly.

Fred Toomey gave Paul a sharp look. He started to say something, but Corey Stuart caught his eye and gave a warning nod.

Once again this made Paul think that the ranger sympathized with him more than the other men did. It gave him the courage to ask for something he wanted very much.

"If you don't mind, Mr. Stuart," he said to Corey, "I'd really like to keep Lassie with me. I'm pretty sure she could be a big help with Comstock."

The ranger gave him a long, thoughtful look that made Paul uneasy.

"She could be a big help," Paul repeated quickly. "With Comstock, that is."

"Yes, with the burro," Corey said. "You will

be back at the camp by night? Definitely. You'll
promise that?"

"Oh, yes, sir," Paul said. "We can make it
earlier than that."

"Okay," Corey said. "And I'm depending
on each of you to keep the other one out of
trouble!"

Fred Toomey gave Paul a suspicious look.
Paul wondered uneasily if the older man suspected anything. But Mr. Toomey said nothing
—then.

When Paul came back from the Forest Service station wagon with the canteen of water
Corey insisted he carry, he saw Fred Toomey
and Tom talking with the forest ranger.

Paul hesitated. It would be possible to slip
around behind the jeep and hear what they said.
He was sure the Toomeys were voicing their
suspicions of his staying behind. Paul wanted
desperately to know what they were saying, but
he could not bring himself to sneak around in
order to find out.

"Don't ever crawl, Paul. Walk right up to life like a man should." Hardrock Hartley's words to him years before echoed in Paul's mind. They beat down the desire to spy and at the same time gave him a simple solution to his problem.

He walked straight toward the three. Intent on their conversation, they did not see him, but there was nothing sneaky about his approach. So it was that he got close enough to catch sufficient words to verify his suspicion that they were talking about him.

"He's wrong if he thinks Hardrock is around here," Fred Toomey said.

"Then let him try to find him," Corey Stuart replied. "It will make him feel better and cause no harm. I think we can depend on Lassie to take care of him."

They looked up then and saw Paul approaching. They stopped talking.

"See you in camp at sundown," Paul said and went on.

He just barely heard Fred Toomey say as he departed, "That boy is stubborn as a burro, Corey—the stubbornest burro in these hills— but I like him."

5   Wild Mountain

WHEN THE OTHERS had gone, Paul tied Comstock's halter rope to a sapling. Then he and Lassie took the trail to Wild Mountain. Soon the trees thinned except for an occasional whitebark pine that struggled for life in the cracks and crevasses of the giant rocks.

Although this was well below timberline, the fierce winds from the Wild Mountain storms had twisted and gnarled the trees.

Ahead, much of the mountain's rocky surface was hidden by thickening clouds. The wind was rising. Water was beginning to trickle in the stone gutters along the edge of the trail, a sure indication that rain was falling somewhere higher up the mountainside.

The rocks about Paul and Lassie were increasing in height. Their fantastic shapes were much like those in Arizona's famous Wonderland of Rocks. One formation resembled the ramparts of an ancient castle so perfectly that Paul almost expected a knight in armor to step out and challenge him. Wind and rain had carved another into a giant replica of an Indian head. Others were simply piled up as if Paul Bunyan had been playing blocks there.

The strong wind moving among the rocks whistled mournfully. Lassie looked up at Paul and whined uneasily.

The boy reached down and patted the dog's head.

"I know, girl," he said, tight-lipped. "If the storm really breaks, we're in trouble. But we can't go back now."

He went on. Lassie hesitated and then followed. She caught the edge of his shirt in her teeth and tugged. Paul shook her off. She turned and retreated down the trail with a happy bound, sure that she had convinced the boy that it was foolish to go on.

Paul stopped, looking after Lassie with dismay.

"Lassie!" he called. *"Lassie!* Don't leave me, girl! Come back, Lassie! I need you!"

"Lassie! Lassie! Lassie! Needyouneedyouneedyou!" The thousands of crevasses and surfaces of the jungle of rocks threw back his words in hollow echoes that made it seem as if the stark mountain were mocking him.

When it was apparent that Lassie was not coming back at his call, Paul turned slowly and resumed his difficult climb up the trail. The way had been cut through the rocks by water pouring down from the stormy mountain for untold centuries.

Beyond the curve of the trail Lassie stopped, waiting for Paul to join her. When he did not do so, the collie whined uneasily and padded back. Instead of rounding the curve, she put her head around to observe the boy.

Paul looked back and saw her. He held out his arms. "Lassie!" he cried. "Come here, girl!"

The dog barked an urgent invitation for the boy to follow her.

Paul shook his head. "No, Lassie," he said. "I know you're right just as you were right before. But this time I can't go back. Hardrock is up there somewhere. If a storm comes, injured as he is, it will kill him, Lassie. Come on, girl! I'm depending on you!"

The collie whined uneasily, but when Paul turned to resume his climb, she padded dispiritedly after him. When she came up beside him, Paul reached down and fondled her tulip ears. Her plume of a tail dragged, and she looked up at him with genuine reproach in her eyes.

Paul looked down at her, almost awed by the way the dog sensed their danger and the almost human way she sulked when he would not go back with her.

Somewhere he had heard that dogs do not have the ability to reason. They learn by rote and then remember past lessons. Looking down at Lassie then, Paul found it hard to believe this.

The dog knew it was wrong to keep climbing these dangerous paths in the face of the approaching storm. Paul stopped. It was hard climbing. He was breathing hard and his legs shook. He had not realized fully until now how much of his mountaineer's stamina he had lost during his two years away from the highlands.

He stooped and took Lassie's head between his hands.

"It's okay, girl," he said. "We don't have much farther to go. The mine shaft is quite a ways below timberline. Even if the rain comes, we can stay inside the shaft until it is over. Come on, girl! I'll bet you a dog biscuit I beat you to the mine!"

But Lassie wasn't buying any of Paul's enthusiasm. She went along because she could not persuade him to go back, but she thought it was wrong. She wanted him to know it.

High on Wild Mountain's summit the storm clouds were growing blacker. Occasional bolts of lightning ripped jagged streaks through their dark folds. Heavy thunder was starting to echo among the rocks.

Paul looked up uneasily, wondering how much farther they had to go. It had been so long since he was here that he could not exactly remember how long it had taken them. Rain was now falling heavily up above. He could hear the roar.

Lassie looked up and whined a warning. Paul set his jaw grimly.

"I'm *not* quitting now!" he told the dog. "I'm sure it is just a little farther. Come on, girl! We'll make it. I know we will!"

He hoped that the next bend in the trail would bring them in sight of the deserted mine. It did not. The boy and dog paused while Paul caught his breath. Before they could start again, the ground started to shake. In the heights above, something started a grinding roar that kept getting louder and louder.

"It's an avalanche!" Paul cried.

Lassie barked an urgent warning.

"You're right!" Paul said. "We've got to get out of here fast!"

It wasn't possible to tell the extent of their danger. They could see only about ten feet ahead because of the masses of rocks. The increasing volume of the roar, however, told Paul that danger was rushing down on them.

He did not think they had time to retreat down the rocky trail.

He whirled about, seeking the easiest way to climb out of the trail's depression.

"Come on, Lassie!" he shouted. "Up we go!"

Lassie leaped atop a giant boulder and, using it as a stepping-stone, scrambled along a ledge of a castle-like formation. Paul came after her. He had difficulty finding handholds in the smooth rock. He grabbed a whitebark pine sapling growing in a split in the smooth granite. It bent almost double under his weight. His shoes slipped on the supporting rocks. He hung by the fragile hold and clawed frantically with his feet for some kind of support.

Below, the trail, hemmed in by the towering rocks on each side, had almost become a river. Mud, dirt, and broken rock churned in a dirty stream of water. The flood was inching higher by the second. Each gully and fissure above was pouring rain into this one outlet.

To fall into that wildly churning torrent meant death! Paul knew it. He looked up desperately. Some dirt hit him in the face. The roots of the pine sapling were loosening. If he tried to pull himself to the boulder just above his head, the force might pull the sapling out. He would fall into the raging water.

"Lassie!" he gasped.

The collie whirled, throwing herself flat on the boulder above his head. Her teeth caught in his sleeve. She scrambled back, pulling with all her strength. It took part of the strain off the pine sapling. Carefully Paul pulled himself up—hardly daring to breathe. Finally he managed to get his foot in the fissure where the sapling grew. Then, with Lassie helping, he pulled himself to the top of the boulder.

For a moment he lay on the boulder gasping. But the water kept rising, splashing and foaming in a wild, churning struggle to get down the steep mountain slope.

Paul struggled to his feet. Above them was a broken stratum of rock which had been heaved upward eons ago when the great mountain was formed. Its jagged face was easy for Lassie to climb, but Paul, nearly exhausted, found it a perilous agony to force his panting, struggling way up it.

Twice, where it was necessary to pull himself to a place above his head, he lacked the strength to do so. Each time Lassie pulled him to safety.

At the top he collapsed beside a twisted dwarf pine that had been deformed in its stubborn struggle to best the ferocious winds that

blew almost constantly near the summit of
Wild Mountain.

Lassie, worried, touched Paul's cheek with
her nose. Paul put his arms about her neck.

"I've only done one thing right since I got
home," he told the collie. "And that was when
I asked for you to come along with me."

Suddenly Lassie pulled back from him, her
head up, ears alert. She looked across the rocks
in the down-slope direction.

"What is it, Lassie?" Paul asked anxiously.

Lassie's tail wagged as she sniffed the air.
She barked, but it wasn't unfriendly. Paul stood
up, looking in vain for whatever it was that had
caught the dog's attention.

"I don't see anything," he said. "What is it,
Lassie? What do you see, girl?"

Lassie barked again. "I don't see—" Paul
began.

Ker-whoom!

The explosion of a rifle cut off his words. A
bullet hit against the rock close to Paul's head.

It ricocheted off with a deadly whine while the violent sound echoed and reechoed among the rocks.

Before Paul could recover from his shocked surprise, there was another shot. Paul threw himself down, taking refuge behind a rock. Lassie crept up beside him.

The strange thing, thought Paul, was that the shot came from the direction opposite that in which Lassie had been looking when she had barked.

After the first flush of surprise Paul felt better. He was sure now that he had found the old prospector. Hardrock, still confused by his lapse of memory, had shot because he had not recognized his young friend.

Paul raised his head gingerly over his rock barricade. Another bullet slammed into the boulder, knocking off chips of granite before it whined off into space.

The next time Paul moved more prudently. He did not raise his head. He moved to the side of the rock and shouted.

"Hardrock! It's me—Paul!"

His only answer was another shot. Paul looked around at Lassie.

"Maybe—maybe it isn't Hardrock, after all," he whispered.

Then who could it be? He raised his head slightly and the quick shot from the hidden rifleman above skimmed practically through Paul's hair. He fell down quickly. The gunman was getting the range. Paul knew he could not risk another look.

He cupped his hands about his mouth to make his words carry farther and shouted, "Hardrock! Is that you? This is Paul! Paul Carter! I've come back, Hardrock. Don't shoot anymore. I'm coming to you!"

"Don't come any closer, you confounded rascals!"

It was Hardrock's voice! Paul went weak with relief. The voice was strained and nervous, but it was definitely that of the old prospector

Paul sought so desperately.

"Hardrock! Can't you hear me?" Paul cried.

"You'll never take me alive!" the old man's voice bawled back at him. "I ain't being strung up for something I didn't do!"

"Hardrock! Can't you understand? I'm not in the sheriff's posse. I'm Paul! I've come to help you!"

Again another shot came in answer. Paul looked at Lassie in despair.

"He can't hear me," he said in a dispirited voice. "The old man is probably getting deaf in his old age. What can I do, Lassie? What can I do? I've got to make him hear me!" Paul whispered in agony.

It hurt bitterly to come so close to doing what he had set out to do only to fail because he couldn't make himself understood.

"We've got to get closer, Lassie," he said to the dog. "We've *got* to! But *how?*"

The rocks rose steep and bare about them. The trail below offered the only easy way up the mountain. And it was not really a trail. It was actually a watercourse through which run-off poured down from the mountain storms finally to join Wild Creek. Centuries of floods had worn its track through the rocks.

He tried to figure Hardrock's exact position. It seemed to Paul that it must be an outcropping of rock similar to the one he and Lassie crouched upon. It was only a short distance away, but separated from them by a deep ravine through which water churned and foamed. It was impossible to get any closer to him that way.

As if in answer to his wish, Lassie started to crawl around the boulder. By going to the right she avoided presenting a target to the mindless man with the rifle.

Paul followed, wondering what she was up to. The hard granite cut into his knees and scraped the palms of his hands, but he did not dare rise up and present a target.

Lassie kept angling forward until she came

to a position where she could not advance without exposing herself. Paul looked at her questioningly. Lassie hesitated. Then she gathered herself and suddenly shot forward.

Paul, still not understanding, jumped up and ran after her.

A bullet ripped through the air, whining a death song as it struck the granite between Lassie and Paul. The dog's sudden dash had taken the old prospector by surprise. He shot late, missing the dog. Then he saw Paul. The boy heard the old man bellow, "I've got you now, you crooked rascal! Blame me for your crime, will you?"

Paul knew he could not get to cover fast enough. Hardrock was a crack shot. He had seen many examples of the old man's fine shooting in the years they had tramped the forest together.

But he ran with all his strength. Across on the other pinnacle of granite, Hardrock Hartley brought the rifle in line with his target.

He did not seem in any hurry. He was drawing a careful bead this time, determined to bring down his quarry.

Paul sucked in his breath with the most awful fear he had ever experienced in his life. It was terrible to be caught under the sights of a man determined to kill, but it was ten times more awful to the boy to realize that he might die at the hand of the man he admired most in this world—a man who had loved him as a son just as he loved Hardrock as the father he had barely known.

"Can't he *see* it's me?" Paul gasped in desperation as he ran for cover. "Hardrock! Hardrock! It's me! It's Paul, Hardrock! *Paul!*"

The old man couldn't—or wouldn't—hear. His gaunt, unshaven face was pressed against the rifle stock. His pain-strained eyes peered straight through the sights—and his finger was tightening on the trigger as he got the proper lead on his running target.

Ker-pow!

The terrible sound of the rifle firing ripped through the rocks, again awakening enough echoes to make the single shot sound like a fusillade.

Paul's foot hit a crack in the granite and he fell. He hit the hard surface with a bang that almost knocked the wind out of him.

For an awful moment he thought he had been shot. Then, in the split second after he fell, he saw Lassie jump back behind the small outcropping of rock that she had reached before Paul.

He knew then that the collie had jumped out just as Hardrock was squeezing the trigger. In offering herself as a target, she had distracted the fugitive's attention. His carefully aimed shot had gone wild as he was startled by the sudden appearance of the big dog.

Paul was slightly dazed, but he had sense enough left to realize that his only chance of living was in pretending to be dead. He sprawled on the rock, his arms and legs outstretched, praying that the injured man would not shoot again.

Ker-pow!

Hardrock fired again. Paul flinched, but the bullet was not intended for him. It went high and wide of both himself and Lassie. It struck the rocks well beyond them.

Suddenly Paul remembered that Lassie's attention had been drawn to something behind them just before Hardrock's first shot. He wondered now if it was at this person—whoever it might be—that the old man had aimed his last shot.

He could not risk moving his head to look. He lay like one dead.

Across the deep chasm that separated the two pinnacles of granite, he heard Hardrock's exultant cry. "Well, I got me one of the rascals, anyway! Let that be a lesson to the rest of you. Follow me and I'll kill you all. I ain't getting strung up for something I didn't do!"

Unable to endure the suspense of just lying

there in the open, Paul slowly turned his head. He saw Hardrock running away. The old man crossed the summit of the pinnacle and started climbing down where a ledge ran along the face of a sheer cliff.

As he watched, he saw Hardrock jump from a boulder to the ledge. It wasn't a difficult jump. But Hardrock's strength and endurance had been sapped by his head wound. He tottered.

Paul jumped up, crying, "Watch yourself, Hardrock!"

For an awful moment the old prospector swayed, balancing precariously. It seemed to Paul that at any second he would slip down into the churning water below.

But Hardrock regained his balance and leaned back against the sheer side of the cliff. He turned and saw Paul. Rage distorted the old man's face when he saw the person he thought he had killed get up. He jerked up the rifle again.

Paul dived for the protection of the outcropping behind which Lassie crouched.

Hardrock's final bullet knocked off half the rubber heel of Paul's shoe as the boy dived for cover.

6   Danger in the Dark

WHEN HARDROCK had scrambled beyond rifle shot, Paul and Lassie crawled from their protecting cover. They could see the old prospector dragging himself slowly along the rough ledge that a glacier had cut probably more than a thousand years ago.

It was easy to tell that the old man had reached a point where he could not keep going much longer. It hurt the boy to see the once-proud, erect carriage now drooping and faltering.

"If we don't get him soon, he'll die, Lassie," Paul said in a stricken voice.

Lassie seemed to understand. She looked from the man to the boy and whined softly.

Across the distance they saw Hardrock pause and steady himself against the granite wall. He looked back and shook his fist at the boy and the dog. He shouted something, but the distance and the whine of the wind among the rocks swallowed up his words.

Paul didn't need to hear to understand. Through his anxiety and worry for his old friend, he felt a surge of admiration for Hardrock's courage. He would never give up.

"And we aren't going to, either, Lassie!" Paul cried, his face twisted with determination. "Come on, girl!"

It was impossible to follow Hardrock directly. Paul decided to backtrack and see if he could find another way across the rocks. The cloudburst on the mountain summit had run its course, and the water of the flash flood was receding, but not enough to permit use of the trail again.

Also, the boiling clouds around the mountain gave warning that another violent rainstorm might be building up. So many ravines led into the trail depression that a flash flood came with each rain. Paul knew that the next time he and Lassie might not be lucky enough to find a way to climb above the churning waters.

They climbed down from the pinnacle, going almost to the level of the flood before they found a ledge that brought them up again on a higher level. Here a couple of short leaps put them atop a jutting mass of rock that the splitting earth had thrown up centuries before. It sloped upward for a long distance. Quite a few dwarf pines struggled for life in its broken fissures.

The giant uplift had a higher elevation than the rocks about it. Paul hoped that the view it gave would help them find a way up the mountain.

The wind was confused and whipped in and out of the rock masses so that it was blowing at their backs as they climbed. Then as they passed a clump of dwarf pines, Lassie suddenly stopped. Her nose twitched as she sniffed the air.

"What is it, Lassie?" Paul asked.

The collie barked and whirled toward the twisted pine which the strong winds had forced to grow almost flat against the rock.

Paul started to call to her again, but then he remembered how Lassie had seemed to catch the scent of someone behind them just before Hardrock had started shooting. In the excitement during the shooting and his anxiety after it, Paul had forgotten the way Lassie had acted.

Not sure what would happen, the boy stooped and picked up a broken piece of granite for a weapon. Then he followed Lassie. She had stopped by the pine. The thick growth was so close to the ground that Paul could not see who or what was hidden behind it. It did not appear dangerous, for Lassie's tail was wagging in a most friendly manner. Paul let the sharp stone slip from his hand.

He came closer and heard a voice whisper urgently, "Go away, Lassie! I don't want him to know I'm here!"

Paul's face reddened with a sudden flush of anger.

"Go away, Lassie!" he said with heavy sarcasm. "We don't want *him* to know *we* know he's there!"

Tom Toomey raised up. He looked sheepishly at Paul and half-angrily at Lassie. "You tattletale," he said to the collie.

Lassie answered the accusation with a happy bark and tried to lick Tom's cheek.

"What's the idea of spying on me?" Paul cried furiously.

"I wasn't spying!" Tom retorted just as hotly. "I believed you were right about too many people going after Hardrock. But I wanted to be along just in case you needed any help."

Paul was still furious, but he choked back his anger. He did not dare start a quarrel now. He did not want Tom to go back and tell the

others that Hardrock had been found. He had to keep the other boy with him now. Hartley had just shown him clearly that the old man would fight to the death.

"Okay," he said, struggling to keep his anger from showing. "You can come on with us." ,

"Come *on!*" Tom cried. "You aren't crazy enough to keep after him!"

"We must!" Paul said, outraged at the suggestion that they should not go on. "He'll die if he doesn't have help!"

"I know," Tom insisted. "But we can't do it alone. We've got to get help. Don't you see, Paul? You were wrong about him recognizing you. He didn't!"

"It was too far away. He couldn't see too well."

"Paul, that isn't so. Hardrock has eyes like an eagle. He could see you, but he didn't know you anymore. It was just like what happened to us at the hospital. He can't recognize *any-body* now."

"I don't believe it," Paul said stubbornly. "He'll know me."

"Paul, you're crazy! If you want to get yourself shot, I guess that's your business. But you will not be helping Hardrock one bit. You can't just walk up and say howdy and bring his mind and memory back to him. That will take an operation."

Paul looked across the wild, broken rocks. He was confused, but still stubborn. At the same time he knew that what Tom said made sense. He was certain that Hardrock would know him, but he was no longer sure what the injury had done to the old man's hearing and eyesight.

"Maybe that's why he couldn't tell it was me," he said aloud. "If I could just get closer. . . ."

"How are you going to get closer?" Tom demanded. "He'll kill anybody he sees coming at him."

"It's not his fault," Paul said resentfully. "He

doesn't know what he's doing."

"I know that—and if you would realize that yourself, you'd know that we must have help to get him."

"What can the rest do?" Paul asked bitterly. "That's why I'm doing this. I think I can do it better alone. I know Hardrock. And I know how he would feel after an operation restored his memory and he found out that he had killed one of his friends who only wanted to help him. That would be awful, Tom. I can't let him kill somebody—you, your father, Corey Stuart, Phil Booth, or any of the others. Can't you understand that? And I can't let Hardrock die up there with his wounds untended!"

"I understand it!" Tom cried. "But how are you going to get close to him?"

"I don't know," Paul said. "But I'm going to keep trying. You know what Hardrock always said: 'You'll win if you keep fighting long enough.' "

"Great!" Tom said bitterly. "But have you

got time to 'fight long enough'? A bump, a fall, or maybe even just the effort of walking can drive that piece of bone deeper into his head. If that happens—well, it's all over, Paul."

"I know that," Paul said, his voice thick with anxiety for his old friend.

"Then you should have sense enough to know we can't wait!" Tom cried. "Stop trying to act as if you're the only one who cares about Hardrock! I care. My dad cares. So do Corey Stuart and all the rest."

"What can they do?" Paul asked miserably.

"Maybe they could distract him. Maybe they could get his attention from in front while you and I and Lassie came in from behind."

"I don't know . . ." Paul said in a whisper.

Lassie touched his hand with her nose. He glanced down and the collie's deep, pleading eyes looked up at him.

"You think I'm wrong, too, don't you?" he asked bitterly. "Well—maybe I am."

"Then let's go back for the others," Tom said

eagerly. "Come on, Paul. Let's get—"

"No," Paul said. "I'm going on. You can go back and bring Mr. Stuart and your dad."

"Why don't you wait—" Tom began.

"You saw him tottering along that ledge," Paul replied. "He didn't look as if he could last much longer. Maybe he can't even last until you get back with the others."

"You shouldn't have come out here alone," Tom said.

"Do you think they would have believed me if I had said he was up here?" Paul asked.

"No," Tom replied quickly. "They were sure he had gone back to the ranch. I see what you mean. If you and Lassie hadn't played your hunch, we would never have found Hardrock in time to save his life."

"So—I'm going on," Paul said. "No matter what happens. I'm going on."

"You're right," Tom said. His face was pale with anxiety and resolution. "I'll go back."

He paused and looked anxiously at the sky.

"It will be dark in a couple of hours," he added. "The clouds over Wild Mountain will make it dark early. But I think I can get everyone here before that."

"It will take you longer than two hours just to walk back to the fire camp," Paul said.

"No," Tom said resolutely. "As soon as I get down to the place that was burned over last year, I'll set a signal fire. There's no chance of the fire getting away from me and spreading there. The lookouts will spot it and call the dispatcher at the ranger station. Then Hank Whitfield will get somebody out to investigate. They'll have walkie-talkie radios."

"I see," Paul said, his excitement rising. "They can alert Mr. Stuart."

"And he can telephone my house. Dad will have to pass there on his way to Hardrock's ranch. Mother can give him the message," Tom added.

"Wonderful!" Paul cried.

Then his face sobered. He shifted his feet,

embarrassed, as if he did not quite know how to say what he wanted to put into words.

"Tom," he said in a low voice, "I'm glad you followed me. And I'm sorry I flew off the handle back there in camp. You and I have done a lot of things together. I should know by now that the two of us can do better than one of us alone."

"It was my fault," Tom said quickly. "I was so worried about Hardrock that I couldn't see your side of it. I do now, and I'm on your side."

Paul stood on the pinnacle of the uplifted rock until Tom was out of sight. Then the boy looked down at Lassie. He had not asked her to stay with him. He would not have called her back had she chosen to go with Tom. It had been her choice alone to stay with him, and he was deeply grateful for her confidence in him, her companionship, and the help she would be to him.

Below, the water was subsiding from the flash flood, but it was still too deep and swift for them to take the regular trail again. They climbed with great difficulty, working their way down and up in a succession of dangerous steps until they reached the ledge where Hardrock Hartley had disappeared.

It seemed like hours had passed since they began to climb. Paul was so tired he felt like throwing himself on the rock and going to sleep. Even Lassie's great strength was taxed by their difficult climb. She padded along silently in advance of the boy, picking out the easiest way she could find.

As they continued, the ledge widened and soon they came to a deep incline trough man-blasted from the mountain. Paul learned later that it had been made to move ore from the mine above.

Fifty years ago miners had solved the prob-lem of getting the ore from the mine to the crushing mill by blasting out this rock flume. The gold-bearing rock was dumped into it, and the ore rolled down the mountain where it could then be conveniently hauled on to the mill.

Steps had been cut along the side for the use of miners to blast out any jams. Paul and Lassie started their weary climb up these steps.

The solid granite now gave way to a variety of rock, including outcroppings of quartz and basalt with occasional traces of what looked to Paul like lava that had squeezed through cracks in the rocks.

Paul could now clearly see the mine tunnel above. It led off a wide ledge back into the mountain. The barren rock strata continued above it for another eighth of a mile, and then the forest took over again with whitebark pine and mountain hemlock bitterly fighting the wind for a chance to live.

Clouds still covered the mountain summit and Paul could not tell exactly how near they were to timberline, but he estimated their altitude at about eighty-five hundred feet or more.

When they finally made the mine ledge, both

boy and dog were glad to rest. They had not caught another glimpse of Hardrock, although twice they spotted his footprints.

From the ledge Paul could see an enormous distance across the Blue River National Forest. Most of it had blended into the blue blur of twilight, although on the mountain the sun was still visible through the clouds. Anxiously Paul searched for sight of Corey Stuart and the Toomeys. He could see no one.

Struggling against disappointment, he turned toward the tunnel, determined to go on.

He and Lassie approached the mine entrance gingerly, hugging the cliff wall. Paul did not want to present too easy a target if Hardrock should see them.

He still was not convinced that Hardrock would not recognize him. They had been so close all their lives and had meant so much to each other that it seemed inconceivable that Hardrock would regard him as a stranger— an enemy.

The sun was gone now. The huge piles of rock below and the forest beyond them were lost in darkness. The mine entrance was a black hole in the increasing gloom.

Paul called Lassie back and inched forward until he was pressed against the rock at the mine tunnel.

"Hardrock!" he called.

Hardrock! The tunnel threw back his voice in an echo.

There was no other sound from inside. Paul shouted again with the same result.

"Maybe he's—passed out!" Paul whispered to Lassie.

Realizing full well the dangerous risk, but determined to take it for the sake of his old friend, Paul went into the tunnel. He knew that anyone inside could see him silhouetted against the twilight sky. He was a perfect target.

He tried to keep Lassie back, but she insisted on coming. Paul exposed himself as briefly as he could. Once inside, he pressed against the rock wall, waiting, listening.

There was no sound—no indication that the man they sought was inside.

"He's *got* to be here, Lassie!" Paul whispered to the collie.

Lassie whined as if in agreement.

"We saw his footprints," Paul went on, trying to convince himself rather than Lassie. "There is no other place he could have gone! He *has* to be in here!"

He raised his voice: "Hardrock! It's me, Paul! Hardrock!"

Nothing answered but his echo.

"Hardrock! Can you hear me?"

When he got no answer, Paul said, "He *must* be unconscious! That head wound finally knocked him out. We've got to get to him, Lassie. Oh, if we only had a flashlight!"

He had some matches in a waterproof container. He carried them as a habit from his mountaineering days. But there were so few of them, he did not want to light one until it became absolutely necessary to do so.

He walked slowly forward. His foot struck an iron rail and he almost fell. It was part of the rusted track laid down for the ore cars.

He steadied himself and went ahead. Then he suddenly realized that Lassie had left his side. He couldn't hear her breathing. Ahead there was nothing but total blackness.

"Lassie!" he cried. "Lassie!"

The collie barked. She had moved much faster than he, and the sound seemed at least fifty feet in front of him.

"Lassie! Wait for me!" Paul called.

He was answered by a sudden flurry of excited barks.

"You've found him!" Paul cried.

He made the mistake of trying to run in the blackness. His foot hit the rusted iron again. This time he fell flat. For a moment he was stunned. He couldn't move.

Lassie was still barking furiously. Paul pulled himself up painfully. "I'm coming, Lassie," he said, his voice unsteady. "I'm coming!"

He stumbled forward, fumbling in his pocket for the match container. What would he see? Fear stabbed through him. Would poor Hard-rock Hartley be lying unconscious and perhaps dead there on the rock floor of the deserted mine?

He hurried on as best he could, guided by Lassie's excited bark. Then, as he got to her, his head suddenly struck something in the dark, and he was knocked to the floor, dazed. He picked himself up, gingerly touching the bruise on his head. He closed his eyes, unable to think for the terrible hammering the blow had started in his badly shaken head.

"What—" he said thickly.

Then, as his senses came back, he struck one of the matches against the striking surface on the waterproof box.

The light flared up, surprisingly strong in the tunnel. Paul gasped with surprise, then shivered with dismay.

Instead of the unconscious man he expected to see, all he saw was a jumble of broken timber support beams, rocks, and dirt.

The ceiling of the mine had caved in, blocking entrance to the back of the mine.

The light in his hand trembled as his body shook. He could tell that the cave-in had not been recent. Rotten timbers had caused it years ago.

"Th-then *where* did Hardrock go?" he whispered in a stricken voice. "He had to have come in here! But he couldn't have gotten past this!"

The match, unheeded, burned down to his fingertips. He jumped and dropped the stem when the flames touched his hand.

"But where *is* he?" he repeated, bewildered and afraid.

7   Lost in the Mine!

HE STOOD for a moment in the darkness, unable to understand where the search had gone wrong.

"I know I saw Hardrock on the ledge," he said, ticking off the evidence in his mind. "Then we saw his footprints in the dust on the steps. That means he must be here. If he had gone back, we would have met him."

The hammering from the jolt he took when he ran into the broken mine timbers so disorganized his mind that Paul found it difficult to think. He shook his head and instantly regretted it. The movement only increased the hammering inside.

Suddenly he realized that Lassie had stopped

her barking. The silence was startling.

"Lassie!" he called.

The collie answered immediately, but her bark was muffled and distant.

"Lassie!" he called again and fumbled for another match.

The light flared up. Again he saw the blocking rubble, but Lassie was gone!

"Lassie! *Lassie!*" he cried in sudden fear.

He heard the collie bark again, but the sound was confusing. He could not place its exact direction.

The match was burning low. He fumbled for another, but before he could light it, he saw Lassie's nose. And then her entire head came into view. She crawled from a hole in the rubble, wagging her tail furiously and barking at Paul.

The match burned out. Paul's hands were trembling so hard that he had trouble striking the next one. He broke the wooden stem of the first match he tried. He struck another. When the flame flared up again, he looked about for something to extend his rapidly dwindling supply of matches. He broke a large splinter from one of the shattered mine timbers. By the time the match burned down to his fingers, Paul had a miniature torch going.

He turned then to Lassie's discovery. Getting down on his hands and knees, Paul saw that there was a low, narrow passageway through the debris that choked the tunnel. It had been cleared by someone. It was not natural. The marks of a hatchet were clearly visible on some of the timber studs. They were not new cuts.

"Hardrock must have opened this tunnel a long time ago," Paul said to Lassie. "But why? The lower shafts are flooded and that's where the gold is. He told me himself that with gold worth thirty-five dollars an ounce, it wouldn't pay to drain the mine."

Lassie barked and started to crawl back through the hole.

"Wait for me!" Paul cried.

He stuck his improvised torch into the hole, carefully looking at the dirt. In crawling through, Lassie had dragged herself in the dust. Still, Paul could make out a few handprints in the dirt where a man had gone through. The prints were so fresh and clear that he was certain that it had been Hardrock.

Then, holding the sliver of burning pine with one hand, he crawled after Lassie.

The cave-in covered about fifteen feet of the tunnel. When he reached the other end, Paul got to his feet. He broke off a bigger piece of wood to start a better light, for his sliver was burning low now.

Lassie raised her head and sniffed the air. Paul looked questioningly at her. She looked around at him uncertainly. It was obvious to Paul that she caught no scent at all.

This, he knew, was because air was being sucked into the mine tunnel from outside. He could feel its pull through the broken places in the blocking rubble.

The strong tug of the wind made him certain that somewhere in the depths of the mine there was another opening to the outside. Otherwise the wind would not pull so strongly.

This made him uneasy, for it meant that Hardrock could well have escaped from the other opening.

"Come on, Lassie," he said hurriedly. "He may not be able to hold out much longer. If he falls, we've got to be there to help him."

He shivered, seeing again in his mind how Hardrock had tottered across the ledge on his way to the mine.

Lassie started down the tunnel, her nose against the ground, trying to track the old prospector. She ran back and forth until she suddenly barked.

Paul followed, running to keep up with her. Then she stopped where the main tunnel branched into two spur corridors.

"What's the matter, Lassie?" Paul asked anxiously.

Lassie whined uncertainly, turning slowly in a circle. Stooping low, Paul could see a confusion of tracks in the dust.

"I guess Hardrock couldn't decide which way to go, either, Lassie," Paul said, his worry increasing. "It looks as if his tracks are going all *three* ways!"

Suddenly Lassie turned up the left corridor. Letting his pent-up breath escape in a rush of relief, Paul followed. They went only a few yards before Lassie whirled around. Paul followed her back to the main corridor.

"He must have started this way and turned around," Paul thought.

Back at the starting point, Lassie again circled around trying to make some sense from the confusion of tracks and scents. Finally making a decision, the collie took the right turn this time.

Paul was certain that straight ahead was the correct way, but he remembered how wrong he had been each of the other times he had disagreed with Lassie's decisions.

The tunnel floor tilted downward. Paul had difficulty keeping up with the dog. He was panting hard. His lungs burned. His legs shook under the strain of trying to go on.

Still he refused to rest. He kept plodding forward. The small torch burned out, leaving them in total darkness. The floor became rougher. Paul kept stumbling as he tried to keep up with Lassie.

Then suddenly he crashed full into the rock wall. He fell, partially dazed. He pulled himself up, leaning against the rough surface of the wall to keep from falling again.

"Why—" he gasped, feeling of the stone. His dazed mind could not immediately understand where it had come from.

He thought at first that the tunnel had ended, but that was not possible or Lassie would have turned back. His head hammered unmercifully from the banging it had taken when he crashed into the wall. He steadied himself and fumbled for a match. He had only three left now.

When the flame flared up, Paul looked around. He saw that the tunnel had ended, but that two more spurs led off at right angles.

"Lassie!" he cried.

From the depths of one of the stone halls came Lassie's answering bark. The sound echoed and bounced until Paul could not tell just where it had come from.

"Lassie!" he cried again. "Where are you, Lassie?"

The collie turned back. Paul could hear her bark more clearly now. The match burned out and there was nothing he could set afire for a torch.

As soon as he could place the direction of Lassie's bark, Paul turned into the right tunnel. The floor here was extremely rough, and the rusted rails of the ore car track had broken in many places. Large rocks were scattered everywhere.

It was almost as if some big explosion or

even an earthquake had ripped through the tunnel in some long-ago day.

The going was hard for Lassie as well as for Paul. This time she did not rush on ahead. Boy and dog groped along together, gingerly feeling their way to avoid possible broken bones.

They had not gone far before the tunnel turned again. Now Paul could see something. There was a break in the mountain, and he could see stars in the night sky.

The starlight at the far end of the tunnel reflected weakly off what appeared to be a lake. A cave-in seemed to have occurred. Piles of rock, debris, and broken timber supports could be seen on both sides of the water.

As they approached the water, the tunnel floor slanted down so sharply that Paul had difficulty keeping his footing. Finally they got to the water and stopped.

"This is the underground flooding which ended mining here," Paul said to Lassie. "The really rich ore veins are under the lake."

Lassie whined uneasily and turned around, sniffing uncertainly. The wind was to their backs, being sucked in from the mine entrance one-sixteenth of a mile back through the tunnels, and was going out the break in the rock on the other side of the underground lake. As a result, Lassie could not get the scent of anything in front of them.

"There must be some way around the water, Lassie," Paul said. "Come on. Let's see if we can find it."

They climbed over a mass of timber and dirt.

"Look, Lassie!" Paul cried. "That looks like a trail someone has hammered out of the rock. It goes right along the wall. . . . It *is!* Come on, Lassie! Hurry! This must be the way Hardrock went!"

Paul started ahead, but Lassie hung back, sniffing the air. The boy stopped and looked back impatiently.

"Come *on!*" he cried. "Hardrock must have

gotten out of the mine through that break ahead."

Suddenly Lassie barked. She started to climb up the debris from the cave-in.

"Lassie! What is it?" Paul asked anxiously.

When Lassie got to the top, Paul saw a hand reach out of the darkness and push her back. The loose dirt gave way under the dog's feet and Lassie slid back down.

"What—" Paul cried. "Hardrock!"

"Don't move! Don't move, you rascal! I got you right in my sights!"

It was Hardrock Hartley's voice, but Paul had difficulty recognizing it. It was strained, tired, sick.

"Hardrock! It's me, Paul! Don't you remember me?" the boy cried.

"Don't move! I'm telling you! If you move one step, I'll blast you all the way to kingdom come!" the old man cried. Despite the hoarseness of his voice, Paul could detect the steel behind it. Hardrock meant business.

"Hardrock! Don't you know me?" Paul cried.

"Oh, I know you!" the old man cried. "I know all you rascals! You'll never railroad me to the gallows for your crime!"

A jolt of fear and helplessness shook Paul. Before, when Hardrock had not recognized him, Paul had believed that it was because of the distance. Now they were not ten feet from each other. The old man could see Paul's face in the starlight. He could hear his voice. But still the boy he had known all his life was a stranger to him.

Paul realized then that the others had been right. The bone pressure on Hardrock Hartley's brain had wiped out all recollection he had of any of them.

"It's just not possible!" Paul whispered to himself. "We knew each other so long and so well. He can't—he *can't* have forgotten all we did together!"

"H-Hardrock!" he said to the old man. "*Hardrock!* Please, try to think! Don't you know me? Don't you know Lassie?"

A shadow passed over the old man's face.
His lips twisted painfully. Paul held his breath,
praying that Hardrock would recognize him.
For a breathless moment it seemed that the old
prospector might. Then Hardrock said harshly,
"Stop that dog of yours! Don't let him climb up
here again. I don't want to hurt an animal just
because his master is a skunk!"

A choking lump came into Paul's throat. He
knew he had failed to penetrate Hardrock's
disturbed memory.

"Come back, Lassie," Paul said in a voice
so choked and strangled that it did not sound
like his own.

Lassie moved over by Paul's side, pressing
against his leg. She looked from the boy up to
the man. Paul dropped his hand down on her
neck, taking courage from her presence.

Warning them that he would shoot if either
moved, Hardrock laboriously climbed down
from his perch atop the debris. He held the

cocked rifle straight at Paul's chest.

"I'm going to tie you up," Hardrock said in his hoarse, sick voice. "You'll be my hostage. If your friends try to crowd me, I'll shoot you!"

Paul stiffened. If Hardrock succeeded in tying him up, it might mean death for both of them. It was very plain that Hardrock, for all his stubbornness and determination, had just about reached the limits of his strength. He might collapse any minute. This would leave Paul bound and helpless, unable to render aid if the old man became unconscious.

And as for the others whom Tom Toomey had gone for, Paul doubted that they would ever penetrate this far back into the mine without someone to tell them that Hardrock had come this far.

Unless. . . .

He looked down at Lassie. If she could get away and guide the others to them—

But he knew that was impossible. If Lassie started to leave, Hardrock would understand that she was going for help. In his disturbed condition, the old prospector might shoot both of them.

"What am I going to do?" Paul thought desperately.

Then Lassie whined and barked sharply at Hardrock. The old man stepped back and stared hard at the dog.

"That dog—" he said, his face creased in painful thought.

"It's Lassie! Hardrock, it's Lassie!" Paul cried. "You remember Lassie!"

"I—" Hardrock began and then shook his head. "I don't remember nobody."

Paul let out a deep sigh of despair. Then Hardrock shocked him by saying, "Tell your dog to go get your friends."

"What?" Paul was so startled by Hardrock's suggesting just what Paul wanted that he was bewildered.

"Yeah!" Hardrock said. "Dogs are smart. Tell her to go get the other rascals."

"Go on, Lassie! Go get Corey Stuart!" Paul cried.

"Stuart? Stuart? I never heard of him," Hardrock said harshly. "Tell her to bring Sheriff Tate and the other crooks! They're the ones I want to be waiting for!"

Paul gasped. He understood now why Hardrock wanted Lassie to bring the others. He knew he should have understood from the beginning, but his head still ached from the bump it had received when he hit the mine wall. He was so tired it was difficult for him to think at all.

Hardrock intended, after he tied up Paul, to lie in wait for the others and shoot them down when they arrived with the dog. They would not be suspecting anything and would run right into the trap.

"Why don't she go?" Hardrock demanded. "Don't you know how to train a dog to mind? Go on, girl! Go on!"

But Lassie seemed to sense that it was wrong

for her to leave Paul. She pressed back against the boy's leg and barked her displeasure at Hardrock.

"Go on!" he shouted and waved the rifle up the tunnel.

"Tell her to go or I'll—" Hardrock shouted to Paul.

"Go on, Lassie," Paul said halfheartedly. "Go, girl!"

The collie looked up at him reproachfully, walked about ten steps away, then turned to look back at them.

Hardrock waved the rifle in the air again, shouting for Lassie to go on. Paul stiffened. The gun was turned away from him, and Hardrock's attention was on Lassie.

He took a quick step forward, raising his arms to grab the gun from the old man's hands. Then he stopped, shaking with fear when he suddenly realized how close he had come to disaster.

He remembered how the Toomeys had said

that Hardrock's trouble was caused by a piece of bone penetrating his brain. It would be impossible for Paul to keep Hardrock from struggling when he seized him. Even in his weakened state, the old man would, and could, put up a fight.

The struggle might well cause the sliver of bone to drive deeper into the old man's head—with fatal results.

"But what can I do?" Paul asked himself in agony.

At that moment it seemed he had no choice but to let himself be tied up as a hostage—which could easily lead to the death of both—or to jump Hardrock and perhaps badly injure the old man.

"Go on, girl!" the prospector shouted at Lassie.

Lassie barked and dropped down to the floor. She put her muzzle across her paws and looked reproachfully at Hardrock.

Paul stepped back. Hartley had not noticed

his slight movement forward. This gave Paul a desperate idea. He thought there might be a slim chance he could get away.

He whirled, running around the end of the cave-in debris in the narrow area between the pile and the water.

"Hey! Stop!" Hardrock bawled, swinging the rifle around.

Before Paul could get out of sight, he fired the first shot. The explosion was thunder-loud in the narrow confines of the tunnel. The slug struck the rocks just behind Paul.

The boy ducked as low as he could and swung under a large mine support beam. Then he rolled to the side and pressed flat against the mine wall.

Here he was outside the area lighted by the shaft of starlight through the break in the mountain beyond the flooded area.

He could see the old man turning frantically from one direction to the other, seeking his escaped prisoner.

"I'll shoot you! I'll shoot you!" Hardrock cried.

And Paul, shivering against the tunnel wall, knew that he would, too.

8   The Capture of Tom

UNABLE TO FIND Paul, Hardrock retreated a safe distance down the tunnel. Lassie padded along with him. Paul felt lonesome and uneasy without his companion. He realized, though, that Hardrock needed her more than he did.

Paul now moved back against the edge of the water. The pile of dirt, rock, and broken timber from the mine cave-in hid him from Hardrock's view.

The light beyond the water puzzled Paul. As he remembered the story of the mine, the shafts descended from the main tunnel deep into the mountain. He had never heard anything about the tunnel running out to another opening.

As he moved along the edge of the water, he

discovered a narrow ledge beaten out of the rock wall. It was only a few feet above the water. In the darkness Paul could not tell where it led, but he suspected that it went around the flooded area.

He started to climb up on it, but stopped abruptly when he heard a noise behind him. He pressed quickly back against the rocks, drawing his body down into as small a knot as possible.

He relaxed only slightly when he saw that it was Lassie. There was a possibility that Hardrock was right behind her.

Lassie came over and sniffed at Paul. Paul put his arm about her neck.

"I'm so glad you came back to me," he whispered. "I need you, Lassie! I need you more than I ever needed anything in my life."

Then Paul straightened up. He wondered what Hardrock was doing, but he did not feel like risking putting his head around the debris to find out.

Instead he grabbed a piece of mine timber sticking from the dirt and shook it vigorously. Dirt and rock cascaded down. The noise of its fall was instantly drowned in the blast of Hardrock's rifle.

"He's watching," Paul whispered to Lassie. "There's no chance of our getting out that way. Come on. I don't know where we're going, but we're going somewhere. Anywhere is better than just standing here."

He climbed to the ledge he had discovered. Lassie leaped up behind him. Paul looked back. The caved-in section of the tunnel still hid them from Hardrock's sight.

Stooping as low as he could, the boy started along the ledge. It was narrow and rough, but not hard to travel. They quickly made their way to the other side.

Here Paul found the answer to the question that had troubled him about the extension of the mine in this direction. He found that the tunnel stopped here. The actual progress of the mine was now straight down through a large shaft that joined a lower-level tunnel. This was now filled with water.

What he had thought was the tunnel running on back was actually a huge fissure—a crack or fault in the rock that ran back to the opening that showed the sky.

The crack did not appear to be new, although it did not seem as old as the mine tunnel. It had definitely been made after the mine flooded and was abandoned.

"An earthquake did it, Lassie!" Paul said to the dog. "Now I remember Hardrock telling me about a quake they had here over thirty years ago. It was the worst in history."

Paul was sure now that it had been this shifting of the earth's crust that had broken the great crack in the rock and also caused the several cave-ins along the tunnels.

As he came close to the break, Paul saw that dirt and rubble had been piled in the bottom to make a walk.

"But why would anybody go to all that trouble?" he asked himself. "Anybody who wanted to get out could go back the other way with far less trouble."

But as he and Lassie got farther into the break, he found his answer. The starlight was now sufficiently illuminating to reveal holes bored along the bottom of the break.

"They're the kind of holes powder monkeys drill for dynamiting rock!" he cried to Lassie. "Somebody has been trying to enlarge this break! It must have been Hardrock. But why, Lassie, why?"

He looked back and caught the faint sheen of starlight on the water behind him.

"Do you think—do you think he was trying to drain the mine by opening a way for the water to get out?"

Lassie was not interested in his speculations. She padded on ahead, leaving Paul talking to himself.

"But what good would that do him?" Paul

argued to himself. "Several mines easier to get to than this one have closed down because they can't mine in this area with gold only thirty-five dollars an ounce. It doesn't pay. Then what reason would he have to drain the water?"

Unable to find a logical reason for what must have been months, if not years, of work in the mine, Paul went on after Lassie. The collie worked her way toward the opening. It was quite a distance—farther, Paul judged, than back the other way to the mine entrance.

As they worked their way along, moving carefully to avoid dangerous falls, the stars were blotted out by the clouds that came and went so suddenly about Wild Mountain. Flashes of lightning ripped across the sky, adding to Paul's anxiety.

Even if he did not come into the rain directly, the difficult climb to the mine had shown him what a storm on the summit of Wild Mountain could do to the trails farther down. He and Lassie had narrowly missed being engulfed in the flash flood on their way up. Then it had been daylight. It made Paul shudder to think what their difficulties would be in the dark.

The lightning increased in frequency and intensity. It ripped across the sky in great earth-lighting streaks, followed by tremendous bursts of thunder.

Lassie was used to mountain storms. She kept padding on, ignoring the weird blue flashes of light that burst in through the crack in the mountain's crust.

Finally they came to the end of the break. Now that he needed the lightning to show him what lay below, the sky stubbornly remained dark. Paul strained to see below, but the darkness was too much for him. The boy sank down on the ledge to get his breath. The mountain air was cold. He shivered even though he was wearing his heavy shirt.

Then the sky suddenly split open with a jagged fork of lightning that seemed to rip from horizon to horizon. Its blue flare brought

almost twilight brightness to the entire landscape.

In that momentary flash Paul saw that the crack opened almost directly over the stark hogback ridge that separated the barren valley from the ranchlands to the west.

Suddenly Paul remembered something one of the men with Fred Toomey had said about Hardrock Hartley, something about the old man claiming to have some scheme to irrigate Desert Valley.

Now Paul understood what was behind all Hardrock's work in the mine. He did intend to drain the water, but not to start mining again. He intended to let it fall down in a waterfall to create a stream he could use to irrigate his desert ranch. Since it stormed almost constantly at the summit of Wild Mountain, water seepage through the rock fissures would keep replenishing the underground lake in the mine shafts. The man-made stream and waterfall would keep running forever.

Paul's thoughts were interrupted by Lassie's bark. It came sharply and insistently from outside the break on the face of the cliff.

Paul yelled back, but his reply was swallowed by a clap of thunder that followed a vivid flash of lightning.

Lassie, thinking something had happened to her companion, came racing back. Then she stood before him, barking loudly. She was so plainly and humanly "bawling him out" for not following her that Paul had to laugh despite the near desperate situation.

"Okay, girl," he said. "Calm down. I'm not going to argue with you. I learned my lesson a long time ago. You're right and I'm wrong every time. What is it now?"

Paul got up wearily to follow her. After a short, difficult climb along the scarred face of the cliff, Lassie struck a well-defined ledge that was almost sidewalk-smooth. A forty-five minute walk brought them back to the area where they had first climbed up to the mine entrance.

Paul started to climb a pinnacle of upthrust rock to see if he could get a line on the men Tom Toomey was supposed to bring. It had now been three hours since Tom had left him. That should be enough time, Paul thought, for the other boy to have signaled the fire camp and brought back help.

Lassie apparently misunderstood Paul's climb and thought the boy was going the wrong way again. She set up a frantic barking to warn him of his mistake.

"Please, Lassie!" Paul called down to her. "I know—"

"Hallloooo!" A faint hail in the distance caused him to break off. He cupped his hands about his mouth and shouted back. There was a moment's silence and then he heard Corey Stuart's voice call, "Stay where you are! We'll come to you."

Paul slid back down the rock, weak with relief. Where, before, he had resented and feared the presence of the others in the search for

Hardrock Hartley, now he welcomed them.

When the forest ranger came into view, Paul greeted him with as much joy as Lassie did.

"We heard her bark," Corey Stuart said, fondly ruffling Lassie's tulip ears. "It scared me at first. She sounded as if something had gone wrong."

"She thought it had," Paul said with a weary smile. "Lassie thought I had made another mistake."

"Tom said you found Hardrock," Corey Stuart said.

"Yes, sir," Paul replied. "He is—"

"Did you find him, Corey?" It was Fred Toomey's voice coming breathlessly through the dark.

"Both of them, Fred," the ranger replied. "Paul and Lassie."

"Great!" Mr. Toomey said heartily. "Boy, you sure gave us a scare. We were afraid you were lost up in these rocks."

"How could I get lost?" Paul asked with a

grin. He reached down and patted Lassie's head. "I have the best guide in the world!"

"Lassie's pretty good," Mr. Toomey acknowledged, "but you shouldn't have come up here alone. It—"

"If Paul hadn't come, then we wouldn't have found Hardrock," Corey interrupted to say. "The rest of us had the wrong idea about where he went."

"That's right," Mr. Toomey said somewhat sheepishly. He held out a big grimy hand for Paul to shake. "Put 'er there, Paul. You were right and I was wrong. And I'm glad to admit it."

"Now what about Hardrock?" Corey Stuart asked.

Quickly Paul told him about their adventure in the mine.

"He has a rifle and he'll shoot anyone he sees," Paul concluded. "There was a time I could have knocked it out of his hand. He was looking at Lassie and ignoring me. But I was afraid of what it might do to his head wound."

"That's going to be our problem, too," the ranger said. "We must take him in such a way that he can't put up a fight. He could be badly, maybe permanently injured if he struggles very much. The doctor made that plain to us."

"How did you two get out of the mine?" Mr. Toomey asked curiously. "You simply said you got away from him. Obviously you didn't come back the way you went in."

"No, we didn't," Paul replied. He told them about the great crack the earthquake had made in the mountain. He also told the two men of Hardrock's work to enlarge the fissure.

"He's bored a lot of holes for dynamite charges," Paul said. "I know he intends to drain the mine to get irrigation water for his ranch."

"He did?" Mr. Toomey said, wonder in his voice. He turned slowly toward the ranger. "You know," he breathed, "it could work, Corey!"

"Yes," Corey Stuart said. "I guess Hartley

knew what he was doing. Just because he got old and cranky, a lot of people started underestimating him. But he was one of the pioneer conservationists in these parts. No one fought harder for soil erosion control and fire discipline than that old man."

"I know," Toomey said. "Hardrock loved these mountains and their trees. He wanted to keep them for the benefit of all the nation instead of for the use of a few."

"And that pretty well sums up what conservation is trying to do. All we are doing today in wisely using our national resources in these forests is putting into effect the very things Hardrock Hartley fought to make people understand even before either of us were born, Fred."

"Yeah, Corey, he is a man we can all be proud to have known. I just hope we aren't too late to help him."

"It's never too late," Paul said quickly. "Hardrock always told me that you'll win if you keep fighting long enough."

"Well, that's a lesson you seemed to have learned well," Corey said with a smile.

"Where is Tom?" Paul asked, looking around.

"When we got to the place where Tom last saw you, we divided into three groups of two and fanned out, looking for some sign," Mr. Toomey said. "Tom and Bob Scott went toward the mine. Phil Booth and—"

Suddenly Lassie barked, looking toward the mine entrance. As if her warning was a signal, there were shouts in the distance. Tom Toomey's voice rang out above the noise and then was lost in the explosion of a gunshot.

Three quick shots followed the first, and then there was confused shouting with the voices blending so that no single one was recognizable.

"Come on!" Corey Stuart shouted. "But watch your step!"

The three set out after Lassie, who was already scrambling over the rocks toward the mine entrance ledge.

By the time they got to the path a man was running toward them. Paul could not make out his face in the dark, but a vivid flash of lightning revealed that it was Bob Scott. The rancher's face was twisted with the effort of running in the high mountain altitude.

He was puffing so badly he could hardly speak when the others joined him.

"He—he g-got T-Tom!" Scott cried. "I-I—"

"Take it easy," Corey said quickly. "Get your breath."

"Hardrock?" Fred Toomey asked, trembling with alarm for his son. "Did he—shoot Tom?"

Scott, breathing heavily, shook his head from side to side. When he could get his breath, he told them what had happened.

As Scott and Tom had approached the entrance of the mine, Hardrock had surprised them by suddenly looming up ahead. He had demanded their surrender. Remembering the wild way the old prospector had behaved in the hospital, Scott was afraid to be taken prisoner.

He broke and ran, dodging like a broken field runner to try to escape Hardrock's shots. He stumbled and fell, dazing himself when his head struck the rocks.

He was out only a moment, but when he got his senses back, Hardrock had taken Tom prisoner. Scott had tried to follow, but Hardrock had retreated into the mine with his hostage. When Scott had loomed up in the entrance, Hardrock had fired at him.

"Come on!" Fred Toomey cried, his voice shaking with fear for his son. "We've got to get Tom away from him!"

"Hold it, Fred," Bob Scott said. "You can't go charging in there. Hardrock will pick you off with the rifle as soon as you show up in front of the mine."

"I don't care what the danger is!" Mr. Toomey snapped. "My son is in there! I'm going in after him!"

"Wait, Fred," Corey Stuart said quickly. "We understand how you feel. We'll get the boy out. Let's see how we can do it without anyone getting shot."

"I'm not waiting, Corey! That's my boy in there!"

"You won't help him one bit by getting shot yourself, Fred," the ranger said. His even tone had a soothing effect on the anxious father. Paul found himself admiring the way Corey Stuart remained calm when everyone else became excited. In more ways than one, the boy found things to admire in the forest ranger.

"I don't think he intends to harm the boy, Fred," Corey Stuart said. "Paul here was his prisoner. What he wants is a hostage to keep the rest of us back. Isn't that right, Paul?"

"Yes, sir," Paul replied. "That's what Hardrock said. And that's what he did the time he was really being chased."

"He's reliving the past," Corey said.

"What are we going to do?" Fred Toomey

asked. His voice was thick with anxiety.

"Let's go up and talk to him," Corey suggested. "Maybe he will agree to let Tom go if we promise to draw back."

"If he hurts my boy—" Fred Toomey said grimly.

"It's not Hardrock's fault," Paul put in loyally. "He doesn't know what he's doing."

"I know," Mr. Toomey said in a dull, weary voice. "I know, but that doesn't lessen the danger to my son. I've got to save him someway."

9   A Defiant Old Man

THEY MADE the slow, weary climb up to the mine entrance ledge. The other two members of the search party joined them. Before they approached the mine, they halted for a conference.

Each of the men had brought a backpack for the climb. When they had left, none of them had known how long he would be on the mountain. To lighten their burden for the coming struggle, they slipped out of the packs and stacked them against the cliff.

"Paul," Corey Stuart said, "you've heard Hardrock tell the story of his escape when he was young?"

"Many times," the boy replied. "It was his

favorite story. He loved to tell it."

"What happened with the hostage he took then?" Corey asked. "Maybe that will give us a clue as to what he intends to do with Tom. He seems to be doing exactly as he did then."

Paul hesitated. He was reluctant to tell them with Tom's father there. He knew it would only arouse Fred Toomey into rash action. As Paul remembered the story, the hostage had tried to escape and was shot down by Hardrock to avoid being smashed in the head with a rock.

The man did not die, but, even so, it was not a story to make Fred Toomey feel easy.

"He tricked them with echoes into turning down the wrong spur tunnel," Paul said. "Then he dynamited the mouth, sealing them inside. They were without food and water. He threatened to let them starve unless they told the truth about the crime they had committed and accused him of. The sheriff, who was the ringleader, wouldn't let any of them talk. Then after two days the rest were so frightened they overpowered the crooked sheriff. Hardrock brought witnesses and got their confessions before he let them out."

"But what about the hostage?" Fred Toomey asked impatiently. "I want an idea what is going to happen to my son."

"I guess Hardrock's idea of a hostage didn't work," Paul said.

"What happened to the hostage?" Toomey demanded.

"He went to prison with the rest of them," Paul said.

"Then he didn't hurt him?"

"He didn't kill him, no," Paul said evasively. "And I don't think he will hurt Tom if he doesn't try to escape."

"Well, knowing Tom—" Fred Toomey said uneasily.

"Yes," Bob Scott said. "That's just what he'll try to do."

"We've got to get close enough so we can reason with the old man," Phil Booth said.

"He's not crazy. He's just lost his memory of recent events. If we can talk to him, maybe we can make some kind of a deal to get him to release Tom."

"How are we going to get that close?" Bob Scott asked. "Hardrock has already shown that he shoots first and then talks."

"I think we can do it with that ore car," Corey Stuart said reflectively. "It's pretty rusty, but I think we can shove it back on the tracks. By pushing it ahead of us, we will have what amounts to a tank to protect us while we get in closer."

He pointed to a six-foot metal gondola set on four small railroad wheels. It was overturned near the mine entrance.

"It'll stop a bullet," Bob Scott said quickly. "It saved me when I ducked around it a few minutes ago."

"We can't go far," Mr. Toomey said. "Didn't you say, Paul, there was a bad cave-in?"

"At least it will get us inside," Corey Stuart

said. "We can't expect to surprise him. All we hope to do is get close enough to try to make a deal."

"What do you think about that, Fred?" Bob Scott asked Mr. Toomey.

"I guess it is the best we can do for now," Tom's father answered heavily. "Don't think I'm blaming the old man, boys. I know it's not his fault. But I must think of my boy."

"We're thinking of him, too, Fred," Corey Stuart said quickly. "If it must come to a choice between the two of them—and I pray that it will not—then the boy comes first. I know that Hardrock would want it that way if he knew what was going on."

"Yes," Phil Booth said slowly. "I think he would, too."

There was room only for the six men to get around the small iron ore car. Paul stood back out of the way while they lifted it onto the rust-pitted rails. Lassie came over and rubbed her head against his leg.

He dropped his hand on her head, but his eyes never left the men struggling with the ore car. His jaw jutted determinedly.

Then he said very quietly, "We can do it, Lassie!"

The collie barked at the mention of her name.

"Shhhh!" Paul said. "Come on, girl. All they're going to do is stir up a fight. They'll kill Hardrock whether they intend to or not. And what's just as bad, he'll kill some of them."

Paul went over to the backpacks, taking two short lengths of rope from two of them. These he spliced together with a square knot. As he got up, he said to Lassie, "Are you with me, girl?"

The collie looked uncertainly from Paul to the men working with the ore car. She whined her concern. Paul felt that she knew what he was going to do and disliked the idea. Once again he found himself surprised at the almost uncanny way she seemed to understand him.

"I know," Paul said. "You're thinking that we couldn't do anything before but run. That's true. But this time it's different. Hardrock's attention will be on those in front of him. We can slip up on him from behind."

"Ho! Easy does it, boys!" Phil Booth's voice broke in.

Paul looked up to see the car slide onto the track.

"Come on, Lassie," he said hurriedly. "We have no time to lose!"

He picked up the piece of spliced rope and, moving quickly now, started back down the ledge. The lightning increased in frequency, and Paul, fearful that the others would see him leaving, hugged the side of the cliff as he hurried away.

Once he looked back. Lassie stood exactly where he had left her. Paul took a deep, unsteady breath. He missed the dog and knew that he might very likely need her help. Lassie would be sure to remember the way. Paul was not so sure he could remember.

Still he refused to go back. He came to the end of the ledge and climbed down the rocks until he found the trail he and Lassie had used to escape from the mine tunnel.

This trip he made better time. Lightning was now flashing almost constantly. One shattering burst of thunder followed another. The momentary flashes of lightning showed huge clouds boiling overhead. Despite his shortness of breath, Paul tried to run. He knew he could expect a cloudburst any moment.

"I've got to get into the mine before it starts!" he told himself breathlessly. "If I'm caught out here. . . ."

He left the rest unfinished, suddenly realizing that what he feared had come true. He was no longer sure of his way!

He stopped, confused. His heart beat wildly. It wasn't fear of what would happen to himself, lost in the coming storm, that shook him so badly. It was fear for Hardrock and Tom. He was absolutely certain that there would be a battle in which one or both of them would be badly hurt if not killed.

"I've *got* to find the way!" he said in agony. "I've *got* to!"

He retraced his way a short distance, trying to find some familiar landmark that would show him the correct turn through the maze of broken rock.

In the weird, dancing light of the electrical storm everything looked different. It was unworldly, like something from another planet.

He stopped again. And then he forced himself to go on. He was not sure he was right, but he had to keep moving.

He went about ten feet and stopped suddenly, listening. His heart hammered and his lungs burned. He leaned against a giant boulder for support. The wind whistled and moaned so loudly through the rocks and fissures that he could no longer catch the sound that had stopped him.

"I guess I was dreaming," he told himself wearily. "I hoped so much she would come that I just began hearing things, I guess."

He started again. Then a break in the wind brought him the unmistakable sound of a dog's bark!

"Lassie! Lassie!" he cried, turning back toward the sound.

He heard her bark again before the wind's roar came back to drown all other sound.

With the wind came the long-threatening rain. The water pelted down in sheets. Driven by the wild wind, it slashed and stung as it slapped the frantic boy in the face.

"Lass—" he screamed, but the wind jerked the word right out of his mouth.

Able to see nothing, he crashed full into a huge rock. He fell and splashed into a pool of water imprisoned between the rocks. He struggled to his feet, now completely confused. He had lost all sense of direction. It was useless to move, for he did not know if he was progressing, going back, or traveling in a circle.

He stumbled around on the lee side of the rocks. This did not get him out of the rain, but it cut some of the cold wind. Paul huddled against the rocks and shivered as the wind drove the cold right through his wet clothes.

Lightning flashed again. During the brief illumination, Paul tried to make out something that would reorient his confused sense of direction. He realized that it was useless. The curtain of rain was so thick that everything was blended into one misty pattern in which nothing was recognizable.

He was so sunk in despair that he didn't bother to look up during the next flash of lightning. So it was that he did not see Lassie until she came right up to his side.

When he did see her, his first reaction was shock. He couldn't believe that she had found him. He dropped to his knees in the swirling water that splashed off the rocks and threw his arms about her dripping neck.

"Lassie! Lassie!" he cried in relief.

The collie jerked away from his encircling arms. Paul understood. They had to get out of this exposed area. He stumbled along, his hand twisted in Lassie's hair to keep from losing her in the darkness and rain, the boy depending completely on the dog's sense of direction.

They had not gone far before they struck the ledge that led to the break in the cliff. They climbed through the break. Paul was still shivering with the cold, but it was a little warmer inside the fissure where the full force of the angry wind no longer slashed and tore at them.

Paul paused for a minute to wring some water from his sopping clothes. This was not to make himself comfortable. Nothing this side of a hot bath and bed could do that. The sopping clothes dripped noisily in the tunnel confines. He knew that his only chance lay in surprising Hardrock. He had to minimize every chance of the slightest noise that might give him away.

Lassie shook herself, throwing a spray of water that caused Paul to say, "You're as bad as the rain!"

They went on, passing along the ledge where Hardrock had drilled the dynamite holes in the rock to start enlarging the crack so the water would drain into the valley below. The sight of the holes brought a new worry.

"I wonder, Lassie," he said to the dog, "if Hardrock has already brought some dynamite down here. If he has—"

Dynamite had played a part in the old pursuit. Then, Hardrock had slowed his pursuers by throwing sticks of it down on them as they tried to climb up the mountain toward him.

The thought of what havoc just one stick thrown down the tunnel at Corey Stuart and the others would do shook Paul with terror.

"We've got to hurry, Lassie!" he whispered.

As Paul's thoughts followed this uneasy line, a flare of light suddenly broke through the darkness of the tunnel. Paul jumped, an exclamation of dismay on his lips. Then when he realized that it had not been an explosion after all, his relief was so great that he felt weak.

What he saw was a fire. And soon the wind coming through the tunnel brought the smell of smoke. They were still too far away to see exactly what was going on.

But he knew there was trouble. He could hear voices now—shouts and wild yelling. The voices bounced off the walls and were distorted so he could not understand a word.

"Come on, Lassie," he said hurriedly. "We may be too late!"

As they climbed along the ledge skirting the flooded section of the mine, Paul saw that the fire came from a pile of splintered support timbers Hardrock had lighted.

Paul could see the old man's silhouette against the flames, but the fire was so bright he could not see beyond it to Hardrock's pursuers.

It seemed that the old man had retreated all the way back to the flooded section to make his stand. He had built the fire to provide light to see his enemies as they came at him. Since he was behind the fire, they could not see him clearly, if at all.

Paul could not see Tom, but he knew his friend was still a prisoner. He was close enough now to make out the voices. Hardrock was yelling that he would kill his hostage if they did not abandon the pursuit.

Paul went closer. Then he whispered to Lassie to stop. Obediently the collie halted and looked up inquiringly at the boy. Paul went ahead, stooping low to avoid any chance of Hardrock's seeing him. He came to a halt back of a heavy beam half-covered with broken rock from the shattered ceiling.

Lassie crept up beside him. Silently the two watched Hardrock. The prospector was standing close to the flames where the fire would shine in his pursuers' eyes. His rifle was half-raised as he shouted his defiance. His face was clearly distinct to the boy. The gray stubble

beard that had grown since he had escaped from the hospital could not hide the deep lines of fatigue and pain dug deep in the old man's face. The once-white bandage about his head was dirty and crooked.

He looked as if he had reached the limits of human endurance. Only a man hardened by years of living in the mountains could have gone through what Hardrock had and still remain on his feet.

Paul looked about for Tom. He still couldn't see his friend.

"Where *is* he, Lassie?" Paul whispered to the collie.

Lassie whined softly deep down in her throat. Soft as the sound was, Hardrock heard it. He whirled around, looking suspiciously in their direction.

Paul flattened out on the rocks, his hand across Lassie's back to keep her from rising. The boy watched in an agony of fear as the old prospector took a quick step in their direction.

Then Fred Toomey's voice yelled out of the darkness, "This is your last chance, Hardrock! If you don't release that boy, I'm coming after you!"

Hardrock whirled around, raising the rifle again.

"Come on, you murdering rascals!" he cried. "I'm ready for you!"

Paul caught the weakness in his voice. It had lost strength in the short time since he and Lassie had escaped.

Then he heard Tom's voice cry, "Don't, Dad! I'll be okay! Don't come out in the open. You haven't got a chance!"

Paul still could not see his friend. From the sound of his voice it seemed that he had been shoved against the opposite wall of the tunnel. Rubble from the ceiling cave-in blocked him from Paul's sight.

"Listen, Hardrock!" Mr. Toomey called, desperation in his voice. "Turn the boy loose and we'll pull out. You'll be free. Nobody will bother you! Please, let him go!"

"You can't bargain with me!" Hardrock bawled back. "You're trying to trick me. I'm not turning my hostage loose. Soon as I do, you'll be right on top of me! I know you murdering rascals! You don't intend to take me back to jail. I'd never get a fair trial. You know I'd expose your rotten conspiracy if I got on the witness stand. You want to shoot me down right here! You want to close the case with a bullet!"

"Hardrock!" It was Corey Stuart's voice.

"Shut up!" the prospector cried. "I'm through arguing with you rascals! If you try to rush me, I'm going down fighting. I'm going to shoot the hostage, and I'm going to get as many of the rest of you as I can. Come on—when you're ready to die!"

Paul felt sick. He shivered and thought, "There isn't a chance. He'll never give up. He's going to kill himself and probably some of the others, too!"

That never-say-die spirit which Paul had admired so much in his old friend was now the very thing that was defeating them.

"I've got to do something," Paul told himself, shivering partly from the chill wind blowing against his wet clothes and partly in fear for both Hardrock and his other friends.

When he had left Corey Stuart and the others in front of the mine entrance, it had been Paul's intention to try to slip up behind Hardrock and bind his arms with the rope Paul had taken from the packs.

It had seemed simple then. Hardrock's attention would be occupied by the danger in front. Paul had expected to be able to slip forward and drop the looped rope over the old man's shoulders and arms.

It did not seem simple now. Several things complicated the plan. The fire gave too much light. Hardrock had stationed himself too far from the rubble pile. Paul could not slip up on him without crossing a wide open area where he could easily be seen. And judging from the way Hardrock had been attracted by their noise before, he was alert to other dangers besides the one in front of him.

"But we must try, Lassie!" Paul whispered to the dog crouched beside him. "There's nothing else to do. No matter what happens, we've got to try!"

He took a deep, unsteady breath and made a loop of the rope.

"Ready, Lassie?" he whispered.

The collie made an uneasy little whine deep in her throat.

Paul tensed, his eyes on Hardrock, waiting for an opportunity to spring forward.

10   "Dr. Lassie!"

PAUL REACHED over and touched Lassie. He took courage from her presence. He did not know what she could possibly do to help him in this desperate hour, but he knew that he wanted her with him.

During these last bitter hours he had learned that she had a way of making things come out right. He did not know what she could do now, but it helped to know she was there beside him.

Apparently someone made a break, for Paul saw Hardrock raise the rifle and fire. The old man yelled in triumph.

"I think I got him! I think I got him!"

"Oh, no, *no!*" Paul whispered brokenly. "If he's hurt someone—"

"Dad! Dad! What happened? Is someone hurt? Please don't rush him. Everything is going to be all right if you'll just wait. He can't keep on his feet much longer!"

It was Tom Toomey crying out. Paul agreed that Hardrock was just on the verge of collapsing. But while that might solve the problem of Tom's rescue, Paul feared that the old man's fall might increase his injury to the point where it would totally destroy Hardrock's mind, if he managed to survive at all.

"No, no one is hurt," Corey Stuart called.

"I'll get you yet!" Hardrock bawled.

He stood well out in the open where they could see him and the rifle now. He seemed to have realized at last that his pursuers were not armed. The movement increased his distance from Paul and made the boy's chance of surprising Hardrock all the more difficult.

"It's now or never, Lassie!" Paul whispered thickly. *"Now!"*

He sprang forward, running toward Hardrock, standing with his back to him. Tom saw him and yelled frantically at Hardrock in a desperate attempt to draw the old man's attention.

In front of the prospector, the men who were barricaded behind cave-in debris also saw Paul and Lassie coming toward Hardrock. They, too, started to shout, trying to rivet the old man's attention.

All they succeeded in doing was confusing the prospector. He whirled, swinging his gun from Tom to Corey Stuart's group. When he turned, he saw Paul running toward him.

Surprise froze him for a breathless second. Then he jerked up the rifle.

Corey Stuart shouted to get Hardrock's attention and started to run forward with the others behind him. Tom was screaming at Hardrock.

The old man refused to be diverted from this new and closer danger. He brought the rifle to his shoulder. Paul was going too fast to stop. And there was no cover he could take. He was in the open between the two piles of cave-in rubble. The fire illuminated him plainly. He was too close to have any hope that Hardrock's shot would miss him.

The others admitted later that they thought it was the end of him. At that moment Paul was unable to think at all. Everything happened so quickly that he was only dimly aware of how close he was to death.

But before Hardrock could pull the trigger, Lassie shot out ahead of Paul. She did not leap with flashing fangs at the old man, as she would a stranger. She hit his legs with her shoulder.

Hardrock stumbled, but did not fall. The rifle jerked up and the bullet intended for Paul smashed into the rock overhead. A shower of broken bits of stone, painful and stinging, splattered the two.

This brief moment that Lassie gave him saved Paul. He was almost upon Hardrock as the old man jerked the gun around to take another shot.

Paul threw the loop of the rope. It went over Hardrock's head. Paul jerked hard. The loop settled and drew taut about the prospector's body just above the elbows.

The gun clattered to the floor and Hardrock threw himself back. Paul braced himself, hanging on to the end of the rope to keep the loop tight.

But the force of the old man's backward movement pulled the wet rope through Paul's muddy hands. He couldn't keep his grip. Hardrock was free again.

The rifle was at his feet. He stooped, pulling at the encircling rope with one hand and reaching for the gun with the other.

Paul grabbed for the end of the rope again, but stumbled and fell. Corey Stuart was racing toward them, but he was still too far away to help.

Paul tried to get up, knowing he did not have a chance. Then he saw Lassie catch the end of the rope in her teeth and spring back.

The loop tightened again about the prospector's body. Hardrock jerked at it, trying to free himself. To keep it taut, Lassie kept backing away. Suddenly Hardrock ran toward her, trying to get enough slack in the rope to free himself.

Paul scrambled to his feet as Lassie jerked the rope tight again. Hardrock stumbled. His hands let go of the rope and went to his head. He swayed.

Paul threw out his arms to catch his friend as Hardrock began to fall. Paul sagged and almost fell himself under the weight. Hardrock was a small man, no taller than Paul, but he was hard and heavy. Paul fell to his knees.

Hardrock was completely limp in his arms. The old man's breath was coming hard and he was making noises like heavy snoring.

Corey Stuart reached their side and helped Paul lay Hardrock on the ground.

"Is he—" Paul asked fearfully. "Have I hurt him, Mr. Stuart?"

"He's unconscious, Paul," the forest ranger said quickly. "You did not hurt him. You saved him from being badly hurt. If his head had struck the ground, there is no telling what that would have done to his injured brain. You did a fine job."

"It wasn't me," Paul replied. "If it hadn't been for Lassie, I wouldn't be here now."

"Yes," the ranger said. "Lassie is a wonderful friend to have around when things are tough."

Phil Booth and Fred Toomey ran to Tom, swiftly cutting his bonds. Corey Stuart and Bob Scott carefully examined the unconscious man. Paul watched them.

"Will he be okay?" Paul asked anxiously.

"I'm not a doctor," the ranger said, "but from what I've learned of first aid, I'd say we had better get him to a hospital quickly."

"That's not going to be an easy thing to do," Scott said. "We'll have to transport him down the mountain by hand. That will take time."

"Couldn't we bring a doctor up here?" Paul asked. "He could operate right here in the tunnel."

"I'm afraid not," Stuart said regretfully. "Even if a doctor could operate here, we would lose too much time going to Black Rock and bringing him back."

"That's right," Scott agreed. "Time is the most important thing now. We'll have to rig up a litter and carry him to the station wagon."

"How is he?" It was Tom Toomey, hurrying toward them. The boy hobbled, his legs stiff and sore from being bound so long.

"We've got to get him to the doctor," Paul replied. "He's still alive. That's all we know."

"He'll pull through," Tom said. "I know he will. And, Paul, I'd like to say I never saw anything braver than the way you and Lassie kept going right into the face of Hardrock's rifle."

Paul was embarrassed. "It was Lassie," he said quickly. "Without her—"

"And she isn't done," Corey interrupted to

say. "Bob, can you get the hand ax out of my pack? Start rigging up a litter. We can use our jackets and weave what rope we have between them. I'm going to send Lassie back with a note for Hank Whitfield."

He went on to say that the collie could get back to camp before they could carry Hardrock down the mountain to where the Forest Service station wagon was parked.

"I'm telling Hank to alert the hospital we are coming and send an ambulance out from town to meet us," the ranger added.

"What about the rain?" Paul asked, his face creased with worry. "The trail down is like a river."

"The rain has stopped," Bob Scott said. "The water runoff goes fast. We'll have no trouble unless there is another squall."

"We'll have to risk that," Corey said. "The way conditions are up here, we can't wait."

The litter was quickly constructed. Hardrock was gingerly lifted into it. Corey Stuart would not let Paul go with them. He insisted that he stay back in the mine until he dried out his clothes. Tom stayed with him.

After Paul had dried his clothes by the fire, he and Tom put out the flames. There was no danger from leaving the fire burning in the tunnel, but both boys were so deeply grounded in the danger of forest fires that they brought water from the flooded area to extinguish the coals.

Then they hurried to rejoin the others. It was slow work carrying the unconscious man down the dangerous trail. Paul and Tom caught up with the men before they were a quarter of the way down the slope.

There was still danger of rain. Lightning continued to flash, and the crash of thunder hammered through the rolling clouds. Occasionally there were a few spits of rain as an added reminder to them not to tarry.

Only two men at a time could carry the litter because of the narrowness of the trail through the rocks. But with each of them taking turns, they were able to keep going constantly.

Paul was so weary he lost all sense of time. It seemed ages before they finally got to the place where Corey had parked the Forest Service station wagon.

They carefully laid Hardrock in the back of the station wagon. Stuart drove slowly to keep from bouncing the injured man any more than necessary. Paul and Tom crouched beside Hardrock, cradling the injured man's head to prevent any bumps that might drive the bone fragment deeper into the old man's brain.

By the time they got to the ranger station, the ambulance had arrived from town. While the attendants transferred the wounded man, Paul —overjoyed to see Lassie again—threw his arms about the dog's neck.

"Oh, you wonderful girl!" he cried. "You never fail, do you?"

The Toomeys and the men with them were to return home in their jeep.

"I'm following the ambulance into town," Corey Stuart told Paul. "I can swing over on the way and leave you at your home."

"I'd like to go to the hospital with you," Paul said. "I can call Mother on the phone. She'll understand. She knows how much Hardrock means to me."

"It's fine with me," the ranger said.

The Toomeys came to say good-bye. Fred Toomey extended his hand to Paul. "Paul," he said, "I must hand it to you. You behaved like a man."

"Thank you," Paul said. "But I didn't—"

Mr. Toomey brushed away the boy's objections. "You proved yourself, and for my money you are going to be as fine a man as Hardrock Hartley. I don't want you to think I am not sorry for him. I am. I admire him. He's more than just a fine man. He was the pioneer conservationist in this area. This entire national forest is really his monument. He was the one who first proposed it and fought all of us for years to get it through our thick skulls that conservation was important."

"That's right," Bob Scott put in. "It was the Forest Service men who brought us soil erosion control, watershed protection, selective cutting of timber, conservation of our national resources, and the multiple-use concept for our forests. But it was old Hardrock who was responsible for starting the drive that made this area a national forest. His is the initial credit. Fred is right. Hardrock doesn't need a monument. This forest is his monument."

When the others had gone and Stuart was ready to start for town, Paul wanted to say good-bye to Lassie, but he could not find her.

"I saw her heading back up toward Wild Mountain," Hank Whitfield said. "She acted as if she were in a hurry."

"Wild Mountain?" Corey said wonderingly. "What could she be after?"

"I know!" Paul said. "We left Comstock up there!"

"Well, from what I've seen of that stubborn burro," Corey said with a smile, "Lassie is badly mistaken if she thinks she can bring her in!"

"Hardrock thinks a lot of Comstock," Paul said. "Maybe I should go after her."

"I think she will be okay," Corey said. "Especially with Lassie along to help as much as she will let her. I was talking with the doctor who came with the ambulance. He says that after this type of operation, it often takes a shock or retraining to bring back the patient's lost memory."

"Oh!" Paul said. "I thought it just came back."

"No," Corey Stuart said. "That is why I want you along. You know him better than anyone. I think you can help there more than any of us."

As they drove into town the sun—not yet risen above the mountains—struck the breaking clouds, setting fire to the sky in a magnificent sunrise.

Paul's heart filled as he watched the great

forest come to light and life.

"I never want to leave here again," he said
to Corey Stuart as the station wagon sped toward Black Rock. "All my life I've listened to
Hardrock tell me about conservation. I understood that we shouldn't let fires start or land
wash away, but I never understood until I went
away to school what a forest really means to
our country."

"I know how you feel," the ranger answered
with a warm smile.

"I've been thinking," Paul said. "I want to
be a ranger like you. I'd be doing the kind of
work that would pay back Hardrock for all the
time and trouble he has spent with me. This
forest is what he's loved and fought for these
fifty years. By becoming a ranger and working
for the conservation that was his dream, I'd be
doing something for him."

"That's a wonderful way to think," Stuart
said. "If you really feel that way, then go back
to college. Study forestry and come back here

to work as a junior ranger in the summers until you graduate."

"That's what I want to do more than anything in the world," Paul said. "How did you get to be a ranger, Mr. Stuart?"

The rest of the way into town Paul listened, enthralled, as Corey Stuart told him about the work of rangers and their struggles to preserve the nation's forest resources. The longer the ranger talked, the more certain Paul became that this was what he wanted to do himself.

When they arrived in Black Rock, Corey ended the talk by saying, "A life's work is not something to be decided too quickly. Why don't you come over and see Hank and me every chance you get this summer? We'll take you around with us. You can really see what a ranger does and find out if you like it."

"Oh, I'd love that!" Paul cried.

His bubbling spirits sank when they went into the hospital. His worry about Hardrock

Hartley, momentarily forgotten, came back with a rush.

The operation was over in an hour, and the doctor came out to tell them that Hardrock was sleeping.

"Will he be—okay?" Paul asked anxiously.

The doctor's face was strained. "Well," he said, "he'll live. Whether he will be the same again is something I can't answer yet."

It was late in the afternoon when Hardrock finally opened his eyes. The doctor came out to get Paul and Corey. In answer to their questions, he shook his head.

"He just lies there and stares at the ceiling. He seems to take no interest in anything. I'm hoping the sight of Paul will jar him out of it."

They went into the room. Although called a hospital, it was just a section leading off the doctor's office and operating room. Black Rock was no longer large enough to support a real hospital.

Paul stopped at the door. Corey Stuart was

behind him. Hardrock turned and looked at them—or rather *through* them, for he seemed not to see anything.

Paul looked around at Corey. He felt as if a great hand had reached inside his body and was squeezing his heart. His lips trembled. The ranger put his hand on Paul's shoulder.

"Take it easy," he said in a quiet, firm manner. "It's too soon to tell anything. He may come out of it yet."

"Hardrock," Paul said, his voice breaking. "Don't you know me? It's Paul, Hardrock!"

The old man slowly turned his head and went back to staring at the ceiling.

"M-Mr. Stuart—I—" Paul began, but he was interrupted by a loud, angry bray outside the sickroom window.

The sound was so unexpected that everyone in the room jumped. But the effect on Hardrock Hartley was the most amazing of all. He tried to lift himself off the bed.

"What was that? What was that?" he cried

in a thick voice, his eyes wild. "That noise! What was that?"

"Take it easy, old fellow," the doctor said, gently trying to push Hardrock back on the bed.

The old man angrily pushed the doctor's hand away. "I want to know what that was!" he cried.

"Open the shade, Paul," the doctor said, worry creasing his face. "We've got to stop his fretting or he'll make himself worse. I don't want to give him a sedative now."

Paul opened the window and started with surprise when he saw Lassie reared up with her front paws on the window ledge. She had the end of a frayed halter rope in her mouth. At the other end of it was Comstock. The burro tilted her muzzle and let out another bray.

"Comstock!" Hardrock cried. The dullness had left his face now. It was weak and drawn but very much alive. "Comstock!"

Paul and the doctor helped raise the old man

to a sitting position and support him there.

"And Lassie!" the old man cried. "It's Lassie and Comstock!"

He turned his head in wonder and saw Paul.

"Paul!" he cried. "Where in tarnation did you come from, lad? And what am I doing in this bed?"

"You took a bump, but everything is going to be all right now," the doctor said.

There were tears in Paul's eyes as he looked over Hardrock's head to the doctor.

"Doctor, you did it!" he said huskily.

"Well, I'll take *some* of the credit," the doctor said with a smile, "but I'll have to share the operation's success with my colleague, Dr. Lassie! It was she who knew what Hardrock needed to jar him back to sensibility. She brought Comstock."

He waved his hand at the dog watching them from the window. "Thanks, Doc!" he said.

Lassie gave a pleased bark, happy because her friends were happy.